Meet My Mom

Dorothy North

Acknowledgement

I would like to acknowledge the help of a few people in completing this creative venture.

Tom Bird and his Write Your Book in a Weekend workshop was where it started and I would never have even thought I could do this if I hadn't tried that. So, I would like to thank Tom Bird, Donna Velasco, and John Hodgkinson for their support during the workshops and after them.

I am also very grateful for the editorial help of Idony Lisle and Bill Worth. They both made extremely helpful suggestions that helped me get the whole thing to make sense.

Finally I need to thank Sue Bowen and Myles Paulson for their the emotional support and feedback. Both are wonderful people who have pretty much literally saved my life. And, of course, my Mom, who gave life to me. I think she would have liked the parts about the babies.

Chapter One

The Bike Ride

My name is Wilma Wilson. Yes, like that Wilma, and please don't, I got the Flintstones treatment a million times from my older brothers plus everyone I ever went to school with. My mother named me after her kindergarten teacher, a family friend who was a lovely woman and lived before the time of cartoons, God bless her. I have grown to like the name, mainly because I am incorrigibly stubborn. This story starts in Possumtown, Pennsylvania, where my Dad bought a cute little farm in 1972 before my thirteenth birthday. Anyway, it was within a few miles of the little town, close enough that we went to school there, rather than the university town that was a few miles in the other direction. It was there that I developed a crush on Rodney Johnson, a quiet kid who was a bit of an unusual target for that sort of thing. My friend had a crush on his best friend Jeff, who was better looking and more sociable. But I always had to be different. Anyway, due to events that I would rather not explain right now, I found myself riding my bike to his house on the evening of Friday, the thirteenth of April, 1973, at about 9:15 p.m. I had become convinced that Rodney and his family were in danger, but at my friend Lucy's advice (originating from her mother Mary, who was a compelling source), I tried to forget about it by watching TV. Specifically, I was planning to watch *The Brady Bunch*, *The Partridge Family*, *The Odd Couple* and eventually *Love, American Style*, which finished at eleven o'clock. I calmed down watching the Brady Bunch, and I got some ice cream when I started watching *The Partridge Family*. These were reruns, so I'd seen the episode already, and it was the one about Shirley Jones being "Mother of the Year." After watching for a while, I put my ice cream away. That was it. The idea of something happening to Rodney's mom without him even knowing, that was just too much for me. No more waiting.

I knew I should look at a map, but I didn't want to bother anybody because it was getting late. I figured I could get to Rodney's house by riding my bike down to the main road to town and taking that to Creek Road, where his house was. My bike was in the barn. My brother Gil was upstairs, and my Dad and Mom were in the kitchen. My brother Rick was either out hitchhiking somewhere or in a mental hospital, I forget which at the time. I quietly picked up my jacket, hoping they wouldn't hear me, and said "goodnight" to them like I was going to bed and then snuck out the front through the living room door. I looked back as I walked to the barn. It didn't look like anyone heard me. I walked my bike for a while along the drive because the gravel might make noise, but finally I started riding. It was a little chilly but once I warmed up, I felt okay. I decided to follow the route of the school bus, heading east toward Possumtown rather than southwest toward the main road.

I felt pretty good passing the first intersecting road, the one that we used to go to the lake. The moon was getting big, and the fields of the farm next door with its early wheat looked beautiful in the moonlight. There was a steep hill after passing that road, but I used the technique I'd learned in last summer's biking group at Girl Scout camp of pedaling hard on the down-slope so I could get as far up the hill as possible, meanwhile downshifting (I had 3 gears) to make it easier to pedal up-hill. I managed the first two hills that way, then I had to get off and walk on the third one, and by the fourth one I was wondering if I was at least halfway there yet. Soon after that I reached the other road to the lake, near where Ron Kramer got on the bus. By then I knew that I really hadn't gotten very far, and I began to realize I was in for a long ride. I couldn't help wondering if I shouldn't have gone the other way. Still, I could always retrace my steps, and it was difficult to feel that bad on such a lovely, moonlit spring night. I liked riding my bike, and hardly ever did it since we moved to the farm. Maybe all the hills had something to do with that. When I came to the crossroads of Old Mill Road, I figured it was a safe bet to turn left, toward the creek and further on, the Turnpike, which I thought would be coming up soon. I was curious what it looked like, riding your bike over it. I was surprised to find that I wouldn't cross the turnpike for some time. But soon, I reached the woods that lined the Creek.

Once I crossed it, I was surprised to see Creek Road right there. *Makes sense that it runs beside the*

Creek, I thought. Since this was the road Rodney lived on, although his house was closer to the main road, I thought it might work to go this way, thinking it might be sort of a short cut. I was wrong about that. It was what my dad would have called the "scenic" route. Right away I was struck by the sight of the old mill house, with sort of a dam in the creek next to it causing a small waterfall effect. In the moonlight it was beautiful to the point of being scary, with the old mill building on the right, next to the creek, and the matching old house on the other side of the road. I was spooked, but I kept riding down the road with the creek flowing to the right of me and some houses to the left, looking like farmhouses, made with stone rather than wood like ours. Farther on, there was a huge farm at a bend in the road that reached on either side, so that it felt like I was riding right through it, wondering how the owners would be feeling about that. But so far, I hadn't encountered any people or cars. Lucky, since I didn't have bike lights, nor a reflecting jacket, nor a helmet. I would never ride like that now. But back then it was different, and I guess I would have felt like a helmet would have made my hair look bad for Rodney. Ironic, because all that riding probably made my long brown hair look a total mess anyway.

The road must have run parallel to the Turnpike for a while, because it was a full half hour before I crossed it. By this time, I was riding for close to an hour, and I was getting tired, not being much of an athlete. Maybe 10 minutes later, I was hoping I was almost there and had ridden the last hill, when I found myself looking at a hill so big it made me want to cry. I didn't even try to ride up this one. When I got to the top there was a pretty brick house to the right. I stood there for a minute, catching my breath and looking down. With the trees not fully grown in yet, I had a sort of a view of the rest of the road to where it met the main road. There were a few houses on either side, nice brick ones, similar to the one next to me, on the left, and on the right, a two-story house with faded white siding and a few outbuildings, and beyond it, Rodney's house, looking shabby and dwarfed in comparison to the others. I had gotten complacent about having the road to myself and was probably standing too close to it, when a light blue truck came careening up behind me and within an inch of me as it passed. *Whew*, I thought, *that was a close one*. Calming down a bit, I noticed the truck pulling up next to the white house, and the man in the truck going in the house. I rode down the hill, not braking too much as my brakes squeaked, and stopped across the road from Rodney's house.

Suddenly I was terrified. How could I just go knock on the door in the middle of the night? It must be almost 11, they might be asleep, unless, like me, they stayed up for *Love, American Style*. In fact, I thought I heard the sound of the ending credits coming from the house.

Just then a car pulled up and two people got out, a woman and a man. It was hard to see clearly, but she looked pretty. Rodney's Mom? The man was taller than she was, with a long ponytail. They were talking for a few minutes, and she started raising her voice. The man yelled something at her, and she yelled back. At this point, I saw the door of the house open and Rodney came out, calling "Mom?"

Then the man put his hands around the woman's neck. I felt a scream coming out of my throat, but I didn't actually hear it. I did hear a shot ring out, and I'm ashamed to say that I had one of my fainting spells. I never did this before or after the age of 12 to 13, but I did pass out sometimes back then, probably a combination of hormones and being skinny from growing six inches in two years (not that I stayed skinny for long). But in any case, I saw the ground come up to meet my face, and that was it for me until I came to and all was quiet. I gradually got up. Fortunately, my bike didn't fall, or somebody might have seen me. In the moonlight, I could see that the woman and man were gone, but I heard branches breaking, and when I looked hard to the right, I thought I could see a big man dragging a body through the woods toward the house next door. My legs were about to give way, so I sat down. Then for a few minutes I thought I was going to throw up, but it passed. What would I do? The best idea was to jump back on my bike and pedal home as fast as I could, and I nearly did it. I thought about *The Hobbit*, one of my favorite books, that I had recently re-read. Bilbo was right the first time when he told them he wasn't going on any adventures. But as the queasiness passed, I realized I had to knock and find out what was going on with Rodney.

When he answered the door, I wished I had gone home after all. I could see he'd been crying, and no boy wants to be seen like that, especially by some girl he doesn't even like. And wow, it was clear at that moment that he didn't like me. I thought he was going to slam the door in my face, but instead he just stared as if he'd seen a ghost, or something kind of worse than a ghost, like a five-foot, six-inch poop monster with zits. Finally, he spoke, "I guess you better come in," with a tone like, Oh God.

Then he said, "Don't look at my Mom," and covered her face with the blanket that was on her where she lay, on the couch.

"She's just sleeping, okay?" he said. But his voice started choking up like he was going to cry.

"What's wrong with her?" I asked, thinking I probably knew what it was but wished I didn't.

"Nothing, okay?" he almost shouted, but with an edge of tears again. This was bad. I didn't want to look at him or his mom, so I looked down the hall, and saw two faces were poking out, a little girl and a boy about three or four years younger than we were.

"Aw," I cried out before I could stop myself. The girl was unbelievably cute, with huge eyes in her little elfin face. Not having any younger brothers or sisters myself, I was always entranced by little kids. Rodney told them, "Why are you up? Go back to sleep."

"What's up with Mom?" asked the boy.

"She's sleeping, that's all. We need to be quiet, so she can sleep," said Rodney.

"Okay," said the boy, doubtfully. Then he looked at me, "Who are you?"

He seemed friendly, with dark brown hair and a big mouth that he appeared to leave open for breathing purposes. Rodney answered, "She knows me from school. She was one of the people who were here yesterday, while you were at Chris' house."

"Oh," said the boy, "nice to meet you. I'm Dan," he waved at me.

"I'm Wilma," I said with a smile. "I want to tell you guys something, but I need to step outside and get some air first. I have this thing where I pass out sometimes."

"Don't do that here, we only have one couch and it's occupied," said Rodney.

I decided not to mention that I had already done so across the street. I went outside and sat on the lowest stair in front of their door. After a few minutes, Rodney came out and joined me. "They're having peanut butter and crackers in the kitchen. That should keep them busy for about five minutes."

"Look, I know this is weird, sorry to show up in the middle of the night like this, but I saw something at the College Library in town about that man who lives next door to you. It looked like he might have poisoned his own parents. He didn't give your mom anything to eat or drink, did he?"

Rodney stared at me for a second, said, "No," and then turned his head. After a minute he said, quietly and slowly, "Look, I really appreciate that you're trying to help. But the best thing you can do right now is just go on home."

"Okay, I get it. I just want to know something. When I got here, I'm pretty sure I saw a man with his hands around a woman's neck. Was that your mom?"

He looked at me, tears in his eyes, "Yes."

"Who shot a gun? Was it that guy next door? Is your Mom really okay?"

He just stared into space and finally said, "Well, maybe I should tell someone. She's dead, and so is the other guy who was with her. I don't even really know much about him, just some friend of my Mom's."

I sat very still, and then I said, "I think I saw that guy from next door, dragging a body over that way. So that body was the man who did that to your mom, and your mom is inside on the couch?"

He nodded, and we just sat quietly for a while. Finally, I asked, "Should we call the cops?"

He said, "See, I don't know. I guess I should, but I don't know what would happen with my brothers and sister, or me. Would they put us in foster homes?"

"I don't know," I said, "Hey, do you hear something?"

There was a noise of snapping branches and breathing. Rodney looked at me and said, "Go inside, quick, so he doesn't see you. Come on," and we both went in the house. He motioned me over to the other side of the couch, to sit on the floor so I couldn't be seen. Then he went outside again, saying, "Hi, John."

I couldn't hear what they were saying after that. Rodney came back in a few minutes and said, "Okay, now he's saying he doesn't want me to call the cops."

"He for sure killed that guy who was with your mom?" I asked.

"I guess so," he said, looking at me with a sort of half smile, "he said that contacting the police would be an unnecessary inconvenience."

I just stared at him and then I started laughing a little. "Yeah, a little inconvenient with that guy's body hanging around, or wherever he is. Don't you think it might be better for you, though, if you called them? That guy is not safe, and here you are with your little ones. We have to figure something out."

He looked away and shook his head. Then he turned back and said, "You know, I could use your help, I guess. Do you mind staying around and helping me with the kids for a while? I don't want them to know about Mom. I'm just going to say she's sleeping."

Of course, I said yes, and that is how I wound up spending that night at Rodney's house, an event that was later regarded with much suspicion. But it wasn't like that, and to explain everything, I have to backtrack a little. It's kind of a long story, but worth hearing, I think.

Chapter Two

Possumtown

In 1972, my family moved to a farm near Possumtown, PA, which was then limited to one traffic light. The main road extended from a nearby town that boasted of a private university with the unfortunate name of Booth, which must have been founded before Abraham Lincoln was president. The road passed some neat residential homes, a nursing home, a few garages, an A&W, and a few roads branching off toward farming country to the North, after crossing the Pennsylvania Turnpike. Running through the farms was Possum Creek, normally a sleepy, brown branch of water about as wide as a road, picturesque and harmless, but during Hurricane Agnes in June of 1972 it became a frightening torrent that flooded many homes. That happened right after we moved there, and the water surrounded the hill that the farmhouse was on, but fortunately didn't get close enough to flood us, apart from the basement.

Maybe because I take after my dad, I understood why he fell in love with the farm, even though my mom and my brothers hated it. Even before I saw the long driveway, I knew I was going to love it. To get there from the main road, you take Church Road down past some houses, over the turnpike and then when you came to the double bend in the road just before it crossed the creek, you knew you were crossing over to magical country. From there, two more turns took you past the Schumaker's dairy farm up the hill, and at the top, there it was, with a view of the mountains, including Waggoner's Gap, in the distance. The driveway was fully a quarter-mile long from the road to the house, and then it curved to the left to go alongside the Creek, which flowed past a cottage with two small bedrooms. Next to the cottage was where a stream met the creek that flowed from Possum Lake, and formed one of the farm's boundaries. This was a good place for fishing, since there were fish in the overflow from the lake that wound up in the stream, but they were mostly catfish and carp, which we rarely ate. The best thing about this little v-shaped area by the cottage, surrounded by flowing water, was that it was just a good place for feeling peaceful and watching the ripples of sunlight on the leaves and the water.

I have a clear memory of sitting right there on my 13th birthday, completely alone, and feeling just fine about doing that. I remember thinking something like, how life had taken me some pretty strange places up to age 13, but sitting there right then, I felt okay about that. Of course, in terms of strange events, I had only experienced the merest beginning, but I wasn't to know that at that time. I was often on my own, since my brothers avoided me, and my mom busied herself making her killer tomato juice. My dad did his work, selling insurance to Air Force personnel at the local barracks and other parts.

Once September came along, we got on the bus to school. It boasted a modern concrete-and-glass building that had TV's in the classrooms where they played the National Anthem and broadcast a waving flag while the kids said the pledge every morning. Prayer was not allowed, but at least one teacher set up a "youth group" where some praying was covertly done, and the administration politely left her alone about this. She bought the kids copies of *The Cross and The Switchblade*, about a young minister who preached to the drug addicts of Bedford-Stuyvesant in Brooklyn. This teacher was a kind woman, and did this with the hope that we students would become good Christians, not with the idea that we might hit the nearest city and start doing drugs, though some may have gotten the wrong idea. Another of the teachers, Mr. Richards, was so socially backward that some of us openly made fun of him, while he took it in stride and remained pleasant. When my friend Lucy mentioned this to her Mom, she said that Mr. Richards had been something of a hero in Vietnam, and that dealing with "you kids" was probably easier for him than dealing with the Viet Cong, although maybe not by much.

In this atmosphere of benign neglect, not much of academic content was learned, but there was a relaxed and friendly tone that may have done us more good than the content of what was presented. My brother Gil didn't like it and begged my dad to send us to school in the other town, but we were living just a little bit too far away to go to the schools there, unless my dad paid some tuition, and he never spent money on us that wasn't absolutely necessary. So, I was going to the junior high school, and my brother was going to the bigger high school at the top of the hill. That meant that we wouldn't have to see each other in school, which was just as well, because running into my brother at school had never been a great idea. I have learned not to take this personally. My parents always made a fuss over whomever was youngest, and I had stolen his thunder when I was born three years after him, particularly since I was a much-hoped-for girl. It didn't help that I was a really cute baby, with blond curls. That was the best-looking time of my life, and by the time we moved to the farm, I was 13, skinny and pimply with greasy hair and glasses, and with not just one, but two older brothers who hated my guts.

Our oldest brother, Rick, was another story. He had been a normal kid, a bit of an athlete and popular in school. He was better looking and more sociable than Gil and me, taking after our mom, who was like a less assertive, brunette Katherine Hepburn. I took after my dad, though without his Paul Newman-like charm, and Gil, well, my mom said he was the spitting image of one of her relatives who none of us knew. But Rick, the oldest, was a sort of tragic hero. Around the time he turned 13, when I was seven and we lived in Ohio, he suddenly started shutting himself in his room, playing the Beatles' *Revolver* over and over again. Gil and I would stand outside and listen, agog. Actually, to me it seemed great that at least Gil was grudgingly willing to spend time with me. We would listen, and sometimes fall into playing air guitar and singing, especially when it came to *Yellow Submarine,* my favorite. One time when we were doing this with extra enthusiasm, Rick threw the door open and bellowed at us like a bull in full charge. We ran away squealing, and when we reached the kitchen, my mom gave us peanut butter sandwiches and a glass of milk. I asked, "Why did he get so mad?"

Mom and Gil just exchanged looks and said something vague, and I forgot about it, not really wanting to know anyway. It wasn't till I was 11 and we were moving to Pennsylvania that I was finally told the truth, that Rick had been diagnosed with schizophrenia and it was a seriously big deal. I could have figured out that something like that was going on, especially when we went to some "family meeting" at the high school in Dayton. I have a vague memory of sitting in a circle and some man I never saw before asking me what I knew about my brother, and my mom sort of butting in and shushing him.

The whole thing made me really uncomfortable, so I chose to forget about it as soon as possible. Then as now, that was my method for dealing with unpleasant things, to ignore and forget. But that applies only to my own life. When it came to other people, I was all ears, especially when that other person was my first big real-life crush, Rodney Johnson.

I say real-life because my first-ever crush was on Jack Wild, who played the Artful Dodger in the movie, *Oliver*. That was the year before we moved to Pennsylvania, when we were still in Dayton, and I somehow wheedled my dad into letting me see that movie something like eight or nine times. I guess I just had to see those big brown eyes again. I especially loved the scene where he first shows up, checking out Oliver before he starts talking to him and they wind up singing, *Consider Yourself.* When my brother showed me an article about a girl in Michigan who'd seen it 15 times, I knew she'd been bitten too. My Dad thought I had a crush on the kid who played Oliver. Nope. Jack Wild was irresistible. I even watched *H.R. Puff 'n' Stuff,* a corny predecessor of *Barney*, just because it had him in it. But I guess I had moved on by the time I started to notice Rodney.

We moved to Pennsylvania ostensibly because my parents thought there would be better help for Rick. That did not turn out to be true, but it later became clear that there was another motive. My Mom had wanted to get my Dad away from a certain woman in Columbus. Problem was, he was always going to find women. In any case, before the farm, we spent two years near Philadelphia, where I was going to a tough school. In seventh grade I got bullied by a couple of kids in my homeroom, almost every day, to the point of tears. By then, I had already come to understand that my parents didn't want me to bother them with that sort of thing, so I didn't, until the year was almost over. My Mom was driving me to school on a Monday, and I told her there were these boys in my homeroom who were saying really mean things to me every day and the teacher just let them. She said, "You know, you're not the only one. There must be any number of kids who are scared to walk into that school right now. But you have to do it."

So, I went, but I didn't think much of her argument. I didn't think she'd ever been bullied like that. Later I found out that, while she may not have been treated that way in school, her older sister had heaped scorn on her in such a way that made Gil's behavior seem like the minor squawkings of a mere apprentice in the art of abuse.

My Aunt Aurelia was a master at bullying, and so were those kids at that school, but looking back, I guess things could've been worse. Still, one of the things I really loved about the move to Possumtown was that the kids there didn't seem to go in for bullying that much. In fact, I was getting along surprisingly well at first, considering what a nerd I was and the fact that I was wearing an *Up with People* button on my shabby navy-blue raincoat all the time. This was from one of their concerts in town that my mother reluctantly took me to before school started and pretended to enjoy, God bless her. I actually did enjoy it, and now that I am getting old, I am willing to admit that, partly with the thought that probably nobody remembers much about *Up with People*. It was like the concert version of *H.R. Puff 'n 'Stuff*, without the puppets. In any case, wearing a button like that made me even more of a target, and yet there was no talk of beating me up. That alone should probably qualify them all for sainthood.

Some of them even seemed to like me, until I asked the guidance counselor why I was in a class level where we were taking math that I'd learned in fourth grade. Not that I cared about math at all, but I did think about eventually going to college, and I didn't want to get too far behind. He admitted that he hadn't checked my school records, and changed me from an average class to a different one that passed for academics at the junior high school. Not surprisingly, the kids in my first class, the one with the fourth-grade math, were annoyed with me for switching, maybe thinking I was stuck-up or something. I got some angry looks and a few insulting letters in my locker. But the mean letters, while they made me a little sad, also brought me a huge sense of relief that if this was the worst they would do, I could certainly deal with it. The great thing was, nobody was talking seriously about beating me up. Meanwhile, I managed to make a few new friends.

One was Mandy, a petite girl with brown hair about the same color as mine. She had blue eyes, freckles, and a fierce sense of humor. When I stayed at her house, we played her records and talked about Rodney's friend Jeff, who she liked, but I didn't have much to say since I didn't really know anybody yet. I think she found me a bit boring. My other friend, Lucy, was also petite, leaving me, at five feet, six inches, to be the tall one who got to reach for things on shelves. She was another brunette but with darker hair than Mandy or I, and flashing brown eyes that rarely missed anything going on around her. She was the only child of older, doting parents who made sure she had everything she needed, while watching everything she did with loving pride. When we hung out, it was always at her house. I had learned early not to invite friends over, because of my brother Rick's unpredictable behavior, but I think Lucy's mother preferred it that way. She let us walk down to the A&W, but that was as far as we got.

My brother Rick went to Harrisburg State Hospital shortly after we began living on the farm. He had been picked up by the police on the Pennsylvania Turnpike, which was only a short distance away, and was hospitalized due to the fact that he was talking in delusional gibberish. We had paid attention to the news that came out around that time, in the early '70s, that schizophrenia was a genetic disorder and therefore neither Rick nor we, his family, could be blamed for it. That was some consolation, although it wasn't clear that the rest of the world was aware of that fact. Around the time school started, we went to visit him. On the way, for a 15-minute stretch of driving on the Turnpike, we were surrounded by a motorcycle gang. It might have been the Warlocks. This unpredicted strangeness may have prepared us mentally for visiting Harrisburg State, which looked like a Gothic red-brick fortress with bars on its windows and the echoes of distant screaming. Inside, it was somewhat homier though a bit clinical. All I remember was that Rick was smiling at us and had an attitude of what seemed like forced cheerfulness, making jokes and laughing. I felt intensely sorry for him, but I couldn't think of anything to say. I just stared at him and the place and tried not to look too freaked out. I thought he was very brave to be smiling at all.

That Monday at school, another girl, who was also new, sat down across from me at lunch. She was pretty, with big blue eyes and freckles. She asked me brightly if I did anything over the weekend. I told her I visited my brother, and when she asked where he lived, without thinking I responded, "Harrisburg State." Her eyes flew open, and then she went back to eating her lunch, silently. I don't recall ever seeing her again. I wondered if she told her parents about it and they sent her someplace else, so she wouldn't have to talk to the weird girl again. It happened early in the year, so it would have been easy enough to start over at another school.

But I stayed where I was, apart from the awkward class transfer, and I grew to like it. I can't remember exactly when I started noticing Rodney. He wasn't in my class, but he did ride my bus. Still, I don't recall noticing him until I was walking around school with Mandy and we ran into Rodney with his friend Jeff, who Mandy just had to talk to. Jeff was a more obvious target for a crush, being taller, with blond hair and the 13-year-old equivalent of chiseled good looks that would be almost hard to look at (without blushing) in a few more years. Of the two, Jeff was by far more sociable. Rodney was so quiet, it was almost like Jeff had a short shadow with darker hair, hazel eyes and pimples. Not to be judgmental, as I was pretty much the Acne Queen of the place. I think it was the running that got my attention. The two of them both ran everywhere, and seemed like natural athletes, but while I recall Jeff at all the athletic events, usually participating, Rodney was never there. I wasn't the inquisitive type, although I loved hearing about people, but my friend Lucy was, and her mom sold Avon. Between Lucy's mom and the ladies at Mandy's church, whom we overheard when we tagged along to church picnics and other events, we began to get a picture of how Rodney and Jeff's families were connected.

Apparently, Rodney's mom had been quite a beauty in the '50s, when she was going to high school with Jeff's mom, and both of them were connected to the same football star, a big guy named John. In fact, there was even another friend of theirs who had a brief involvement with the same guy. This was Mandy's nice aunt Donna, our favorite of the ladies at church. In fact, she was the one who filled us in on some of Jeff and Rodney's family history on one of those picnics in the Spring of that year, 1973.

This was not long after I had been given some unpleasant news. Since my Dad had originally insisted that we were staying on that farm for good and never moving again, he let me decorate my own room, with lace curtains and flowered wallpaper and a row of books on the wall. I loved it, and the farm and my little group of friends at school. But that Spring, I found out we were moving again after all, at the end of the school year, so I had to start preparing myself to leave my nice new home. I alternated between pretending it wasn't happening, to slamming doors and throwing books, but nobody really cared when I did that, so I stopped bothering.

Some mornings, though, I used to get up while it was still dark and walk over to the barn. I sat at the edge of the barn where it opened toward the East, and watched the sky gradually grow lighter over the creek. I couldn't actually see the creek, since it was lined with a thick covering of trees and bushes, and there was a steep hill on the other side, so you couldn't really see the sun come up. But the sky went gradually from dark, to gray, to ever paler gray, until the beams of gold could be seen from the direction of the hill, and then the sunlight gradually painted everything with the palest gold and pink. And that, I felt, was the most beautiful thing I ever got to see. The stillness and quiet was gradually filled with birdsong, and the background to that was the faint hum of grasshoppers and bees, and the leaves moving, and the water flowing, and it all blended in a prayer of hope. And I thought that maybe it could be okay that I was leaving, as long as this beautiful beginning still happened on this one little patch of land.

Chapter Three

The Church Picnic

The day I rode my bike to Rodney's house was April 13th, a week before Good Friday. So, I guess it was a couple of weeks before that, when I went to Mandy's church with Lucy. Mandy told us we should come because there would be a picnic after the service, for people to talk about the plans for Easter over some nice food, coffee and amazing cookies. Lucy's mother drove us but didn't stay, going off to do her grocery shopping and pick us up when she was done. We sat with Mandy and her family, and after the service we heard the folks at the church discussing their preparations for their annual Good Friday procession parade and the Easter pot luck after church. Lucy and I had promised to tag along for the parade, although we were secretly amused that the church's Rev. Smith, who had to be pushing 60, would be playing Jesus, as he did every year. Nobody else seemed to find that funny, which spoke to how beloved this kindly and jovial man was by his congregation. The church was a modest brick building with one stained glass window of an angel in the back, and a much-abused wooden belfry in the front, with a sign by the door, Possumtown Lutheran Church. This was the main church people in Possumtown attended, unless they drove to town like my parents, or went to the Baptist church. I am not sure, but I think the Catholic church was in town. My parents took us to a Presbyterian Church, but I usually dragged my feet because it wasn't the same as the church we went to in Philadelphia. That was the only thing about Philadelphia I really missed. Of course, some lucky kids at our school didn't go to church at all, because their hard-working parents didn't have the money or didn't feel like it, or both. Lucy's mom was one who didn't feel like it, but she was happy to drive us there. This was a great way for me to get out of going to my parents' church, too. Lucy and I really liked going to that Lutheran Church, with Mandy and her family, and Lucy's mom was always there to pick us up when it was over.

She would come in to look for us, meanwhile having a chat with Mandy's mom and other people there without having to sit on those hard, wooden pews.

At the picnic, Mandy's Aunt Donna greeted us with a beaming smile, her blonde hair pulled back on the sides into a large blue barrette on the back of her head, in a blue tunic-style pantsuit and turquoise jewelry. She overheard us talking about Mandy's crush on Jeff.

"I knew about that, God bless her. I was friends with his mother, you know," she said, between puffs on a Virginia Slim. "The three of us were friends, me, Denise, who is Jeff's mother, and Miranda. Miranda had a bunch of kids, what's her oldest's name, he would be about your age. Oh yeah, Rodney."

Hearing that got my attention. "Jeff has a friend named Rodney, they're always together," I told her.

"Really? That's interesting, probably the same kid, with a name like that. But I don't think their mothers talk to each other much these days. In fact, the only reason I hear from them is because I insist on calling them at Christmas. Seems like a good time for old friends to get in touch, don't you think? Except it's hard to catch either of them sober, and half the time Miranda doesn't even have phone service.

It can't be easy for her, living on disability with all those kids. Not that it's totally my business, but I have to ask you, does Rodney look okay? I'm always a little worried about them."

Lucy and I looked at each other, and I blurted out, "He's skinny. We don't eat lunch at the same time, but he doesn't look like he's eating enough, and he wears these dirty, worn-out clothes, and the same sneakers all the time."

Lucy rolled her eyes at Donna and Donna giggled. "Somebody else has a little crush, huh? Well he's probably cute if he looks anything like his Mom. She was always the beautiful one, with her long chestnut-colored ponytail and her big, pretty hazel eyes. She was the one that football guy really liked, that guy John, that Denise was always after. Too bad for Denise, he was crazy about Miranda, and she wouldn't even talk to him. Me and Denise both got involved with him, unfortunately, though in my case it was just kind of an accident."

Lucy's eyes gleamed, and she smiled at Aunt Donna as she asked, "How was it an accident?" This was something she had to know. Aunt Donna gave her a look of combined annoyance and resignation, and sighed.

"Okay, I'll tell you about it, but only because I want you girls to pay attention and don't be naïve like I was. It's kind of a long story. See, when we were sixteen Denise got a car, and drove us out to a diner in town where the football players got together to drink in the parking lot. That guy John was there, showing off and yelling at people. He kept looking at Miranda, but she wasn't impressed. Denise noticed this and gave me a look, and I guess we were staring at John. Finally, he came over and asked us how we were doing.

We said fine, except for Miranda, who wouldn't look at him, as usual. Then he told her, 'hey, if you're not having fun, I could take you somewhere else.'

I think Miranda just got up to go to the bathroom, without even looking at John. She was like that when he was around. Probably she even stopped to talk to that other football player, the one who she wound up getting married to. His name was Dan, I think. He was nice but didn't look very smart, what with being a mouth breather and having tons of acne, but she didn't seem to care. Anyway, John looked mad, and asked us what her problem was with him."

"Wow," said Lucy, "this guy really couldn't take a hint."

"Yeah," I said, "if she didn't like him, why couldn't he just leave her alone."

Aunt Donna just looked sad. "He wasn't the kind of guy that leaves people alone. But Denise, God help her, she liked him, a lot. Some girls really like men who are mean and can't behave themselves, and Denise has always been like that. So, she said something to John about how Miranda didn't like it when he acted mean sometimes, but it didn't bother her. Or something like that. Such a dumb thing to say. I was trying to be helpful, even though I didn't really like the guy, and I said something about how he should try acting nicer to people when Miranda was around, if he wanted her to like him.

And then dumb Denise started telling him how great he was in the football game they played that afternoon, even though he practically killed some poor guy, making it sound like he'd done something good. And John probably said how he hoped he didn't put the poor guy in the hospital for too long. He used to say that a lot, bragging. He was so mean. Denise didn't get that, or maybe she really didn't care. Either way, she tried to get him to take her out instead of Miranda. He said he would, and she went to her car to get her sweater, and on her way, I remember she was walking kind of slowly and moving her hips a little, like Lauren Bacall in that movie, except Lauren Bacall looked good doing that, but Denise just looked dumb."

"I saw that movie," I said. "Lauren Bacall was so beautiful."

"Well, don't you try to walk like that next time you see Rodney, Wilma. You'd probably fall over," said Lucy, laughing.

"And if you tried it, you'd look like a duck," I retorted.

"I never saw that movie, so I don't know what you're talking about," said Lucy, shrugging. "Anyway, I want to hear the rest of this. Sorry, Aunt Donna, tell us what happened. Did he take her out?"

"No," said Aunt Donna sadly, "I wish that was the way it ended, but no. As soon as she was gone, he was telling me how he needed to talk to me about Miranda. I told him we better wait till Denise came back, but he kept insisting, he needed to talk right away, and we had to go over to his car so we could have some privacy. I tried to tell him that Denise liked him, but he said she wasn't his type, and please wouldn't I talk with him about Miranda for just a little while, and finally I said, okay.

And that was the wrong thing to say, for sure. He said we had to sit in his car to talk about it, and once we were in that car of his, he wanted to go somewhere quiet, and why I didn't just say no at some point I will never understand. Anyway, he wound up dropping me off home in the early hours of the morning, telling me he would call me the next day. I wasn't even positive I knew what happened, but I was, for sure, sorry that it did. So, after that, not only did he not call me, but he was telling stories about me to other boys, who were staring and giggling. To make it worse, Denise was angry with both me and Miranda, and that was the end of our friendship, as it was at the time."

Donna took a long pull of her cigarette and looked thoughtful. Finally, she said, "Girls, never get into a car with a football player unless you are totally sure about what you are doing. And that's the truth, like that lady on Laugh-In used to say." She put out her cigarette and stood up.

"Where's Mandy? Oh look, she's talking to a boy. Isn't that what you girls should be doing?" she winked.

"Well, Wilma won't be interested if it isn't Rodney," said Lucy, and I shoved her.

We went to talk to Mandy, who was just talking to Ron Kramer, who sang in the school choir with me. He was great to talk to, but we just regarded him as a friend who sometimes gave us useful, boy-related feedback about things. When he saw us coming, he wandered away toward the dessert table. He did seem to get shy when Lucy was around. "Your Aunt Donna is cool, Mandy," said Lucy.

"Yes, she is," beamed Mandy. "Did she tell you about the Catholic Worker house where she takes care of old winos? She loves to talk about that."

"No, we were pumping her for information about Jeff and Rodney. She was friends with their mothers," said Lucy.

"You mean, she *is* friends with them," corrected Mandy. "They just aren't much of friends. They like to drink," she finished in a dramatic whisper. "My mom said once that it was no accident that Donna takes care of alkies now, since she got started doing that in high school."

"Wow," said Lucy, "who knew that a boring looking kid like Rodney could have such an interesting mom."

"He is not," I interjected, but she ignored me.

"She was a beauty with some football star after her, plus being an alcoholic, whoa," said Lucy.

"Not just that," said Mandy, "that same football star practically raped my poor Aunt Donna, and she said Jeff's mom was involved with him too, and he might even be Jeff's father," she finished even more dramatically.

"Could he be Rodney's father too?" I asked, getting a bit carried away.

"No," said Mandy, "Rodney's mother hated that guy."

"Oh yeah, Donna said that," I agreed.

"Well, aren't you sorry we were talking about Jeff and you weren't there?" said Lucy, and Mandy blushed and said, "Shut up."

"Look, she's blushing. I don't know which of you guys is worse," she added, and kicked my foot slightly.

I pushed her shoulder again, and she started laughing. "Come on, you guys," said Mandy, "they've got tons of cookies over here."

Chapter Four

More About Going to Church with Lucy

Lucy's mom, Mary, was a big woman with a big, friendly smile, unless she felt like you might present some kind of threat to her daughter, and then look out. Those eyes, so friendly, could turn into deadly torpedoes from a wall of stone. This I saw once when she was at school, talking to a teacher who gave Lucy a grade she didn't think was fair. I really didn't want to ever get on her bad side.

Their house had two stories, with two or maybe three bedrooms. Lucy's room was next to her parents' room. We got used to keeping our voices down, but if there was anything important to talk about, like boys, we took a walk to the A&W. We didn't buy anything, just walked there and back, partly for the exercise because, like any 13-year-old girls, we were always thinking about losing weight. And this is how we had our conversations about Rodney, and Jeff, and some guy Lucy liked for a while whose name I forgot.

The following weekend after the picnic was two weeks before Easter, if I remember right. A whole week before my bike ride over to Rodney's house, and I still had no idea that I would ever think of doing such a thing. Lucy and I were walking that Saturday afternoon, so she could update me on some important information. "So, here's what Mom heard, from some neighbor lady who lives on the same road as Rodney, you know, where he jumps off the bus and goes running, probably to get away from you."

"Shut up," I said, "What did she say?"

"He has at least three, maybe four, little brothers and sisters, at least one of them is a baby, and they hardly ever see his Mom. He takes them all to the store every day. Can you believe that? They walk, all of them, to the store, to get some groceries and come home. Without the Mom. Couldn't they go once and just have stuff for the week?"

"Maybe because they have to walk, they can't carry that much. Why can't his Mom drive them? Or his Dad?"

"I guess his Dad either died or left. My Mom didn't hear about that. But the neighbor did say she thinks the Mom drinks."

"That's what Mandy's Aunt said too. But you know, my parents both drink but they can still drive to the store. That is weird. Poor Rodney," I went on, "do you think they have enough money for food? Are they hungry?"

"I don't know," said Lucy thoughtfully, "his clothes are kind of messy too. I guess this is why. The things you don't know about people."

"I wonder if we could do something?" I said, not sure how that would work out.

"Well, it would look weird if you just went up to him in school and handed him a sandwich. Maybe we can think of something. Let's ask Mom if she knows about something we could do."

We went back in the house. Her mom had grilled cheese for our lunch, and it smelled amazing. She also poured coffee for us. She made her extremely tasty percolator coffee, and she gave us evaporated milk to put in it. She often made it when I was there because she knew I loved it. She had these thick white cups that I think were made of glass. It was all perfect.

"Thanks so much," I beamed, taking a cup. I felt funny when I used her first name, which was Mary, but she didn't want me to call her Mrs., so I just avoided saying it.

"That's okay," she said, smiling back, "Did you girls have a nice walk?"

"Yes," I said, and after a moment's hesitation and looking at Lucy, I blurted, "Lucy said somebody told you something about Rodney. He rides my bus. He always jumps out and runs flying down the road, I think it's Creek Road."

"To get away from you, like I said," giggled Lucy. I made a face, and then I continued.

"We feel bad, wondering if they have enough to eat. Do you think there's something we can do?"

"Hmm," said Mary, "people don't always like it if you just go handing them food. The church that Mandy's family goes to has a food donation project going on. Maybe you could talk to the minister, why not? Just ask him to keep it quiet so you don't offend anyone."

"He could use some help with his clothes, too," added Lucy.

"But there again, you don't want to go upsetting people," said Mary. "You gotta be careful how you do these things. I go into a lot of people's homes around here, and you'd be surprised how many could use some help. But they won't ask. Sometimes, though, I can get away with slipping them something if I do it the right way. You remember, Lucy, how I gave a bunch of your old clothes to that girl down towards Waggoner's Gap?"

"Yeah," said Lucy, "it was kind of weird to see her come to school in my clothes, but it's a good thing to do anyway. We don't have clothes for boys, though."

"Wilma, maybe your brother has some old clothes to get rid of? That might work for Rodney. Meanwhile there's all those younger kids. Let me think about that, some of my customers might have a few things. You girls can go to Mandy's church tomorrow and ask the minister, he's so nice. I'll drop you off and pick you up again."

I piped up, "My Mom could probably pick us up if you want."

But Mary responded, "No, it's no problem for me to do it. I'm happy for the chance to show up and say hi to them, without having to sit through the service. Those pews are too much for my backside."

Mary was always happy to drive us, which was a big difference with my parents, who tended to sigh and complain. Although my Dad had been happy enough about driving me to town to volunteer at the McGovern campaign office back in the Fall. Probably not every town in Pennsylvania had a McGovern campaign office, but this one did because of people who worked in the college. Not that I cared at the time, but I don't remember seeing many student volunteers, maybe just a few. The office was run by some motivated college faculty members, who I vaguely remember to have been thirty or fortyish. Maybe my Dad enjoyed talking to them. I wasn't paying attention to that, and I was kind of surprised it didn't bother him to drive me, especially when I asked to do it just about every day toward the end of the campaign, in late October and November. Well, he was no fan of Nixon, and I guess he wanted to do his part. Besides, it may have given him a chance to drive to the barracks to talk to potential life-insurance customers. It was an indication of how nice the kids at the school were that nobody picked on me for wearing a McGovern button, even though everybody else's parents were voting for Nixon. A few kids did tease me in a friendly way, which was fine with me. One kid even called me "Nixon nose," because my nose does in fact have a ski slope shape similar to that famous one. Since he was a boy who seemed to like me, I was happy to respond with fake annoyance and make it our little thing.

The church service that weekend was not exactly riveting, but I was used to that. Back in Dayton when I was eight or nine, I had refused Sunday school and elected to brave my way through the service with my dad. I can't remember why but I'm guessing that Sunday school was an even bigger bore. It went fine the first few times, I even sat quietly while my dad took communion, until the fateful day when my friend Linda from school, who had also refused Sunday school, probably for the same reason, was sitting next to me. In fact, we had been given an entire pew to ourselves, which was a serious mistake. Linda was a cute little girl with pretty brown hair and eyes, but she liked a joke. She would whisper something funny, made even funnier knowing we weren't supposed to laugh, but I was able to repress it until she stuck two rolled-up programs into her dress and said, "Lookit my boobies!" pushing them this way and that, a la Jayne Mansfield. I collapsed and laughed till I wept, and the elderly ladies who were sitting in front were appalled. One of them pulled me aside after the service and told me that she would complain to the minister. Having no idea what the minister thought about anything, I didn't really care, but I was mysteriously excused from church after that, much to the annoyance of my older brothers who had relished their Wilma-free time on Sunday mornings.

Back to Possumtown. In a smaller church with friends around me, one of them from a family who was close to the minister, a kind man who always said hi to everybody, it was easier to behave well. Reverend Smith was middle-aged, paunchy and balding, but his smiling, good natured demeanor was what you noticed first. His wife had mild cerebral palsy, walking with a limp. She had a gray braided up-do, and her speech was slow and sometimes difficult to understand, but it was always clear that she had boundless good will toward whomever she was talking to, and focused her entire attention on them, regardless how trivial their concern might have been. I figured she knew what it felt like to feel bad and not be able to get anyone's attention, and

I loved her, as most people did. She often carried a shawl, pulling it around her on chilly days, but there was nothing cold about her personality. Many people in the church owed their sanity and ability to continue coping with their difficult circumstances to her unwavering attention and concern.

Since many were struggling financially, there was a regular program at the church to provide extra food and clothing or other needed items, which she supervised. At the end of the program each week, there was a list of the current needs of the congregation:

"One church member has a broken refrigerator. Requesting donations if anyone has a spare or knows someone who does."

"Two bicycles needed: Girl age eight, boy age twelve."

"Don't forget our toy store." This last was a collection of donated stuffed animals and dolls, given to children on request. There was also a small "library," less popular but no less important to the children. Radios and musical instruments were also given sometimes, depending on what was available. They got donations from a few bigger churches in the vicinity, and a few local families who were lucky to be better off. Lucy's mother was a frequent donor of clothes, since she spent most of her Avon money dressing Lucy up. My clothes were worn to a threadbare state before I gave them away. It was a fact that we didn't spend much on clothes in my family, apart from my Dad's suits, which he needed for his job, I suppose. Lucky for me, I didn't usually care, and in fact I'm still most comfortable in jeans and a t-shirt. But it was a different story for girls who wanted to wear something nice that their parents didn't have money for. Mrs. Smith, at the church, was there looking out for them, and the little ones who needed toys and books, and other folks who needed something, like a new fridge, in a hurry. She managed all of this with some help from some of the women. It wasn't an easy job, but she accepted it all with a smile. There were some members who tended to take rather a lot, but she usually ignored this. She and Rev. Smith reasoned that they would get more from somewhere, and it shouldn't be prevented as long as there was enough for everybody. They never discussed politics, smiling and changing the subject, or occasionally reminding people that it was all in God's hands. I was pretty sure that they had liked my McGovern button, but nothing was said, and although people assumed they were Republican like everybody else in those parts, nobody, as far as I knew, could recall them ever discussing it.

Mandy went to say hi to Reverend and Mrs. Smith after the service, and we trailed along after her. We said hi to them, and then I said to Mrs. Smith, "Lucy's mom said you guys have a program for giving food and clothing to people? There's a boy at our school who might need help…"

I trailed off, and Lucy added, "We don't think he would accept anything from us, though. We wondered how we could get him some help without being obvious."

"Best way," said Mrs. Smith, "would be for him to just come and get what he wants. But if you can't get him to do that, well… Do you know where he lives?"

"Wilma, did you ever happen to notice which road it is that he runs down to get away from you?" asked Lucy.

"Shut up. I'm not sure. It's either the second or third stop after we reach the main road, on the bus. Okay, second stop."

"Creek Road or Old Mill?"

"Not Old Mill Road. I guess it's Creek."

Lucy turned to Mrs. Smith. "We think he lives on Creek Road. Can't be that far down from the main road, but we're not sure exactly where."

"That's okay," said Mrs. Smith, laughing, "I think we have a member who lives near there. I'll give her a call. In the meantime, you don't have to mention it to him. He may have a lot of reasons for not wanting to receive help from you girls at school. Just being a friend can be enough, you know."

"Thanks so much, Mrs. Smith," we beamed at her. It was a relief to leave the problem with someone who seemed to know what to do. When I got home, I turned on the radio and forgot about it, until I heard them say this: "Who remembers the court case of John Smith? A guy out Possumtown way who killed a guy, actually someone he knew, and tried to make it look like a suicide. This guy who did this just got released from jail about a week ago and has been seen in the area. An address was given on Creek Road… just a minute…okay, maybe I wasn't supposed to say all that. I just thought people should know. By the way, this one's for you, John. This song was originally recorded by the Crickets after Buddy Holly died," and there were the opening bars of *I Fought the Law* by the Bobby Fuller Four.

Chapter Five

Fried Chicken

It was the first time I ever really listened to that song, later recorded so memorably by the Clash. I sat stunned, thinking, Creek Road is where we were saying was the most likely location of Rodney's house. What if he really does live there? Like I always did when I needed to talk to someone about something, I called Lucy.

"Did you hear that thing on the radio about the guy?" I blurted out, and she finished my sentence, as she often did.

"On Creek Road? Yes, and I was thinking about how you must be freaking out if you heard that. I kind of figured you might call me. Well, we still don't know for sure that that's where Rodney lives. But if it is, then wow, it would feel weird to have a murderer living near your house. Do you guess he listens to the radio? I wonder if he heard that?"

"Should we say something?" I said, suddenly even more nervous about that idea.

She laughed, "Why we? I think you should do it, finally talk to the guy. It's time you did that, Wilma."

"How am I going to do that? Jeez. You have to at least come with me."

"Wouldn't miss it for the world. I have to go, Mom wants me to help her with the potatoes. See you tomorrow," she said with a lilt in her tone that conveyed she knew I was petrified.

I got off the phone and went upstairs and sat on my bed. I was mad at myself for being scared of talking to Rodney. This is not how women behaved in the books I read. They either went after their men confidently, like Scarlett O'Hara, or waited for the man to pursue them, like Arwen in *The Lord of the Rings*. Or what about Jo in *Little Women*? She was a little bit more complicated. She went ahead and talked to boys, but she didn't yell at Laurie when he fell in love with Amy, or flirt openly with Professor Bhaer. How did they know what to do? I felt inadequate. But I should make sure he knew about John Smith. I knew I would feel even worse if I thought he didn't.

I went downstairs where my Mom was fixing dinner, roast chicken with rice and ratatouille from the fresh farm vegetables. I still can't make ratatouille, feeling sad for all the times she went to the trouble of making it and we just gobbled it up ungratefully. Unlike Lucy's Mom, my Mom rarely asked for help. I think doing it helped keep her mind off Rick. She did let me help chop the vegetables sometimes though, so I started doing this now. I asked her, "Mom, did you hear anything about some guy around here who had killed somebody and recently got released from jail? It was on the radio."

"Oh, you know I don't listen to that. Really? Don't the police know about it? Don't worry. Did you do your homework?"

"Yeah," I lied.

She just said, "Okay. Help me set the table," and I went to do that. We had an actual old-fashioned polished wood dining table in the next room, with matching chairs, from my mom's family, and real plated silver. My Mom fussed how the sulphur in the local water made the silver tarnish. Rick was either gone off or in the hospital again, I couldn't remember which. I had learned not to pay too much attention, just responding to whatever my mom said about him with "uh-huh," but not really thinking about it. It was easier that way.

Lucy and Mandy used to question me about Rick, but they eventually gave up. Mom had made me promise not to talk to people about Rick, and I didn't, apart from that one time with that new girl when it just slipped out. I couldn't help noticing that Mom would talk to people about it whenever she felt like it, but I never brought it up. There were loads of things we were not supposed to talk to Mom about, lest her resulting bad mood brought fearful consequences to all. Once in a while, I would tell her something anyway just to see what she did, and when she got upset, my Dad gave me the silent treatment, which was not really so different from how he usually acted, and my brothers heaped scorn on me for breaking the "Don't Tell Mom" rule.

I still wanted to talk to her about Rodney, but I didn't want to tell her too much. While I was formulating a question in my mind, my brother Gil came in and said, "Mom, Cheesie got out again. I think she's headed for the Schumakers' farm."

Cheesie and Moony were our two heifers, now almost grown to cow-hood, who were bought in response to the meat crisis, with the goal of eventually having them slaughtered and keeping the frozen meat in the back of the house with all the frozen and preserved vegetables, to be retrieved and turned into steak or stew or whatever during the winter months, or whenever. There were a bunch of things wrong this idea, one of which was that we weren't likely to eat that much beef and probably some of it would go bad. Particularly since my brother Gil turned vegetarian in response to this situation, leaving only me and my parents to eat it all, and I didn't even like steak that much, although I loved my mother's beef stew. They had been really cute heifers, but that wouldn't have kept them from becoming beef. But Cheesie was at least partially solving this problem for us by removing herself from danger.

Mom said, "Look, dinner's almost ready. When your Dad gets back, we'll tell him to call the Schumakers."

"That's great," I said, "remember when Rick was here, and one of Dad's clients called, and Rick picked up the phone and said, he can't talk to you, he's out chasing cows."

Gil just heaved a sigh and ignored me. Most of the time, he pretended I wasn't there, unless he was mad at me. So, I tried to ignore him back, but sometimes it wasn't easy. Unlike me, he was popular in school and teachers liked him. He even had some big role in *The Sound of Music,* the high school play that year, though I forget who he played. Other kids would ask me about him. I said as little as possible, not wanting to admit that he didn't really talk to me.

Forgetting about asking anyone about anything, I ate my food and went upstairs to get back to my reading. I was plowing my way through *The Lord of the Rings*. I'd read *The Hobbit* at age 10 or 11, but couldn't get into the trilogy until that year in eighth grade. It helped with the adaptation to the new school and surroundings, to escape to Middle Earth for a bit. Being on the farm could lend itself to pretending as I walked around, that the Creek was the Great River, or that the little group of pines on the hill was Weathertop, where Frodo was wounded by the King of the Nazgul. I liked to imagine as I read what it would be like to be one of the characters, but in *The Lord of the Rings* the only women were Arwen, Galadriel and Eowyn, and I could only relate marginally to Eowyn, who was at least human, and not at all to the beautiful elf ladies. I had to invent one of my own, a sometimes bumbling but well-meaning female scout, sort of apprentice ranger and wizard, or at least apprentice to a lesser wizard in case Gandalf didn't have time for me. I would show up here and there, helping the hobbits and others on the side of the Fellowship as best I could. Thinking on this, I pondered, how would such a person respond to Rodney's situation? Surely, she would think of something to do.

I can't just go up to him and start asking him stuff. I can ask about the radio thing, okay, because I would like to make sure he knows, but I can find out other stuff on my own. I will look at the paper when my Dad gets home with it and see if there's anything there. Or maybe Lucy's parents have it? How can we look up old information about that guy? Maybe there would be something at the library. Meantime, I called Lucy again.

"Do you remember the name of that guy, the murderer who might be living on Creek Road?" I asked, purposely avoiding mentioning Rodney.

"No, but maybe my Mom does. Mom. Wilma wants to know who was that guy…yes, I'll ask her… you know, the guy who murdered somebody? Oh,

John Smith. His name is John Smith, isn't that funny? Like the guy who married Pocahontas."

"Wait a second. Aunt Donna said the football guy, the one that liked Rodney's mother, was named John. Couldn't be the same guy, could it?" I asked her, my mind spinning around this idea in sudden panic.

"That would make it extra creepy. Let's hope not. Maybe we can ask Mandy, her Aunt Donna would know."

"Do your parents have the newspaper?"

"They might. Mom…" Lucy was listening. "We have to wait and see if Dad brings it home. We don't get it delivered. Mom wants to know if you can come over for dinner Thursday, she's making fried chicken, and we know you love it."

"Great!" I said, "hey, do you think we could go to the library after school? I want to see if there's any old newspapers available with more information about that guy."

"Gosh, you mean the library here in Possumtown? They don't have much, but we could try it. Mom, can we go to the library Thursday after school?" There was a longer pause.

Lucy was back. "She says we can only go for an hour or maybe a little less because the chicken takes time and she can't make it ahead, it has to be fresh. Does that sound okay?"

"Yeah, all we have to do is ask the librarian about old newspapers. It shouldn't take long. Is it a good library? I've never been there."

Lucy said, "I've only been there once, for a few minutes. It's kind of small, you know? I mean, it's really just a bunch of bookshelves in somebody's house, but they're working on making it bigger. It's not exactly state of the art. I don't know if they'll have what you want, but you can always go to the college library."

"Okay. Maybe I'll ask Mom or Dad about that, if they can't help us. I don't really feel like it, but I guess I will try to talk to Rodney about that guy tomorrow. Seems important, now that he might even be the same guy who used to know his mom," I said.

"I almost forgot about that," said Lucy. "Are you really going to talk to him? Hey, don't do it if you don't want to. I was kidding. I'm sure he would have heard about it by now anyway."

"Probably he has," I said, feeling better. "Well, we'll see what happens. I better go. See you tomorrow."

"Hey, Mom says to tell your Mom thanks for letting you come Thursday, and we will get you home after dinner."

"Okay, I will," I said, suddenly remembering that I hadn't asked her yet. I went downstairs and asked her, and she said sure. She always offered to do some of the driving, but we all knew Mary would do it anyway, so I just let it slide. I went to bed thinking about the library. I mean, if I found out something that I needed to tell him, I could still do it Friday. If I didn't find out enough, I would have to ask Mom or Dad to drive me to town, and then it would be a problem, because who knows how long it would take for them to get around to that. But, hey, maybe if we could convince Mary that it was important, she would take us. That was a comforting thought.

The next day being Wednesday, I did think about talking to him, but the opportunity just never came up. Thursday, I ran into him and Jeff on the stairs, but I got nervous and dropped my book, and I just couldn't get the words out. Some Middle Earth scout I would have made. Still, it would be helpful to know more about that John Smith guy. Hopefully it would not be anything much, just your average murder case, whatever that was. But when we got to the library, no dice. The librarian said that records like that were kept on microfiche, rolls of film that could be looked at using a viewing screen, and they didn't have that in Possumtown. She was sure the library at the College would have it. But as we were leaving, we saw Reverend Smith and his wife walking up. Lucy scurried over to them.

"Reverend Smith, Mrs. Smith, it's so nice to see you out here. This is my Mom," she gestured toward Mary, "and you know Wilma. Are you going to the library? We just came out."

"Great," said Mrs. Smith with a smile, "Did you find anything good?"

"Well," said Lucy, "We wanted to look at old copies of the newspaper to see if there was anything about John Smith, you know, that guy who just got out of jail?"

"What a shame that they broadcast that information," said Mrs. Smith. "How can rehabilitated criminals get a break when everybody knows what they did and where they are?"

"Ordinarily, I would agree with you, my dear," said Rev. Smith, "but as we both have reason to know, this is no ordinary case, at least, not for this community. She is being generous to him because he is my nephew," he said, looking at Mary. "To me that makes the matter even more serious. It's true that he wasn't well treated as a child, and we probably should have intervened more. I was serving a church in Chattanooga at the time, that's where we got the idea for the toy store and church library, so much poverty there. Although to be honest, we prefer to serve in poverty-stricken areas, since that seems to be our calling. But it always felt better to be here, where my family is from. My wife's family is in Ohio."

"Really?" I said, "we used to live in Dayton."

"Cleveland," she smiled.

"Anyway, by the time I was here and available to him, he was already the high-school football star and not interested in talking to his uncle, the minister. Sadly, my nephew murdered someone who lived right here in Possumtown, who'd been a friend of his in high school, played football together and everything. There was drinking involved, and the victim had a wife and children. I believe they still live around here. Poor thing must have been devastated. What was the name? Oh yeah, Johnson, I think."

I gasped and blurted, "Rodney's what, his father, was murdered? So, he is the same guy Rodney's mom used to know. And the guy is supposed to be living somewhere near where Rodney lives."

I looked at Rev. Smith and then at Mary. Mary stared at me, apparently thinking. Finally, she asked me, "Do you know where this kid lives?"

I said, "I know what street he gets off the bus, but I'm not sure which house." Of course, this was the day before I wound up riding my bike to Rodney's house. At this point, I still didn't know where he lived, but I was about to find out.

"Would you girls be okay with driving down there and taking a look? Maybe we could just make sure he's okay," said Mary, looking a little surprised to find herself saying that. She looked at Rev. Smith as if to confirm what he thought.

"Actually," said Rev. Smith, "that would set my mind at rest too. Would you give us a call and let us know what happens? I should really go myself, and I will plan on visiting them soon, but this is a busy time for us with Easter at the end of next week. Even so, next week I will do it. Monday, hopefully. But I would be so happy for you to let me know how they are. Please call us," and he looked at Mary earnestly.

"I will, Rev. Smith," she said with one of her big smiles, and shook his hand. We all said our goodbyes and left. We took off down the main road, looking for the intersection with Creek Road, and turned left when we found it. I wasn't sure at all how we would know which house was Rodney's, and Lucy seemed suddenly very thoughtful, like she wasn't sure she liked doing this. But her mom had such a look of determination on her face that there was no thought of suggesting that this might not be a good idea. She said, "We'll just drive up as far as someone would be able to walk, and then we'll try to see if there's anyone outside."

So, we did that, and it seemed like we drove a really long way without seeing anyone at all. We were giving up, on our way back to the main road, when we saw Rodney in front of a house, talking to some big man with a beard. As we got out of the car and approached them on foot, we could see that he looked uncomfortable, maybe even scared, but that was nothing compared to the look of shock on his face when he saw us. He just broke off talking and stared at us, mute. Finally, the man turned and saw us, and smiled, reaching out his hand to Mary, saying "Hi, I'm John Smith."

She almost flinched, but then composed herself and shook his hand calmly, saying, "Mary Hanson."

"Are you girls friends with Rodney here?" the man asked, in a friendly tone.

Rodney just looked at us; we stared back. The man with the beard looked a little uncomfortable, then laughed a little. "I just moved in next door about a week ago, and came by to say hello to Rodney's mother, but I guess she is indisposed."

Mary gave him a serious look, then looked at Rodney. "Is your mother all right? Could I talk with her?"

Rodney finally spoke. "No, she's sleeping." He looked at us with a total lack of comprehension, as if we were from Mars. Mary addressed John Smith, "Well if she's sleeping, then you're going home, right?"

He looked a little pained, but nodded and said, "Yes, I was just going to leave. Nice meeting all of you, Mary, girls. Rodney, looks like you're doing alright in school," he grinned, then headed home. We watched him for a minute. The yards were fairly large and there were trees, but we could make out the two-story house and pale blue pick-up truck.

"Is that the guy who was in that story on the radio," whispered Lucy loudly, her eyes open as wide as I'd ever seen them. Rodney winced. I finally asked him, "You knew about that?"

He said, "Well, only about six people came up to tell me about it in school."

"Okay," I said, looking away.

Mary suddenly looked intently at him. "Are you all right, young man? You have everything you need right now?"

"Well," he said, with a long sigh, "It looks like my Mom had a seizure yesterday, but she's okay now. She just needs to sleep. Thanks anyway."

Mary asked Lucy, "Do you have a pen and paper, honey?"

Lucy fumbled in her pocketbook. It was a cute little navy-blue leather-look number from Mary's Avon collection. "Here Mom," she said, handing her a pen and a small spiral notebook with a blank page. Mary wrote, then handed Rodney the paper.

"Here's our phone number. Call us, okay? I want to know if that man comes and bothers you, or anything else you might need. Anything, you understand? And we're coming back Saturday with some extra food and clothes for you guys. How many other kids with you? Three or four?"

"Uh huh," he said, taking the paper and looking confused. "I got a little brother who's at his friend's house right now, and this is Nina. Get inside, Nina," he said somewhat brusquely as the little girl poked her head out the door.

Lucy and I went, "Aw," at the same time, and Mary leaned toward the girl with a big smile and said, "Well how are you, sweetie? Aren't you the cutest thing, all eyes, and that hair would be beautiful if we got the chance to brush it. How old are you?"

"Four," said the girl in a barely audible, high-pitched voice like the beautiful little elf-child that she appeared to be. She looked like she liked the idea of having her hair brushed.

Rodney said, "Well we certainly thank you and I'll tell my Mom when she wakes up. I'm gonna go check on her now. Sorry I can't invite you in," saying this last with a firmness that even Mary couldn't shake. He smiled at her, but the look he gave me was not appreciative.

Mary smiled back and said, "Okay then, see you soon," and we walked slowly back to the car. Lucy was totally silent, but her eyes were still wide, while Mary's smile had disappeared, a look of grim resolution replacing it. I just stared numbly at the trees on the other side of the road from the houses, a thicket of trees with pointed leaves that I vaguely recognized, I think my Dad said it was some kind of birch, with some pine and a bramble of weeds making it almost impassable. Finally, I looked at Lucy and tears came to my eyes. "Don't worry," she said, patting my shoulder, "he looks like he's basically okay," but she spoke slowly, searching for the right words.

Mary just stared straight ahead without a word, opened the car door and said, "Get in, girls."

We went to their house in silence, only breaking it when we were helping with dinner in the kitchen, dipping chicken pieces in batter and rolling them in flour before Mary put them in the frying pan.

Mary said, "Now, Saturday, we're going to make a whole bunch of this fried chicken again and take it to their house. Wilma, I'm sure you'll want to come along."

I nodded my head, and started blinking back tears again. This time Lucy smiled and said, "Wilma, just wait till we see them when we bring that chicken."

"They will be like little terriers," chuckled Mary.

I smiled, wiping my eyes, and said, "and I bet you he will still hate me."

I looked at Lucy and we both snorted at the same time, laughing so hard I almost knocked over the bowl with the batter in it. "Careful," said Mary, but she was laughing too.

Next day being Friday, the school was in a cheerful, elevated mood, but we didn't see Rodney anywhere. Finally, our friend Mandy cornered his friend Jeff after lunch, so we went up to them. I'm not sure Mandy liked that, but I ignored her and asked him, "Where's Rodney?" and then suddenly felt embarrassed for having asked.

But he was concerned, too. "I don't know why he isn't here. He called me about his Mom having a seizure, and then later he said she was okay, and then he called even later and told me about that weird neighbor of his, and how you guys showed up. He was sure surprised about that," he said, looking at me with a sort of guffaw.

I looked away, embarrassed again, but thinking. "Did he say anything about why he's out? Is his Mom sick again?"

"I don't know," Jeff said, shaking his head and opening his steel-blue eyes wide.

Mandy gasped a little. He smiled at her, and said, "Well, I'll call him when I get home. If I hear anything before that, you girls will be the first to know," he said, looking at me with a sort of smirking expression.

I let it slide, having no idea what to say anyway, and as he walked away, Lucy said, "Well, I guess that's that. Let's find our next class. Oh Mr. Richards, that should be entertaining," and Mandy and I groaned.

Chapter Six

The Problem

The problem was, once I have an idea in my head, I find it hard to let it go. I am still like that. My brother Gil, God bless him, after some years of restlessness, eventually took to meditation like a duck takes to water and became a priest. At his suggestion, I tried meditation, but it didn't work for me. Thoughts dog me and won't let go. Now that I'm old, that makes me neurotic, but in a young person it can be a kind of strength, especially if they find a means to express or even act on their most compelling intentions.

Back then, I thought I wanted to look at those microfiches at the college library, even though I only had a vague idea what microfiches were. After I got home, the bus ride seeming so dull without Rodney and his baleful looks, I was after both parents to take me to the college library. Mom was involved in putting partly cooked tomatoes in jars, but my Dad was weakening. Possibly it was the thought of pretty young librarians, or maybe he had clients to see, like back in the McGovern days. So off to town we went, getting there at about 4:30, half an hour before closing. Once the pretty librarian got my Dad to shut up, she showed me where I could find the town's newspaper microfiches from 1962 to 1965. Then she showed me how to use the machine to view them, which wasn't difficult once she got me started. This was the right time window, and I did indeed find a series of articles about John Smith's murder conviction. The last one especially caught my eye, with a couple of paragraphs in smaller print on a different page. Here was information that made me really queasy: "Smith's parents died in 1962 under somewhat suspicious circumstances, with an appearance of poisoning that was not confirmed by autopsy. Smith, however, was not a suspect, being in military service at that time."

Still, I didn't like the way that looked, having read some murder mysteries, such as my Dad's copy of *The Moonstone* and some books of Poe that my brother Rick used to have, so that it seemed possible to me that poison could be administered slowly or possibly left somewhere to be innocently taken by accident at a later time. I wondered about John Smith's interest in Rodney's mother and her subsequent illness. *Could he have poisoned her? I couldn't help wondering to myself, and if he did, what could happen to Rodney and his brothers and sister?*

I honestly had no idea. A vague notion of orphanages crossed my mind. I shuddered. It seemed to me that Rodney needed to know, as soon as possible, to keep that man away from his family. As much as the paper had said there was only a suspicion, I just felt sure that the man was capable of having done it, and that he could do something similar to this innocent family. Why would he want to hurt them, though? Maybe he was still angry that Rodney's mother didn't like him when they were in high school. I remembered hearing about that from Mandy's Aunt Donna, and I was thinking that might be why he had killed her husband, Rodney's father. But the point was, how could I let Rodney know that they might be in serious danger?

The thought briefly occurred to me that I could try telling my Dad about this and get help from him. He could just drive me over there and let me tell Rodney quickly, and then get home for supper. Somehow, I knew this wouldn't happen, but I decided to try him anyway. Problem was, I didn't get my nerve up to ask about it until we were on our way home in the car, and that may not have been the best time.

"Dad, I was looking at the microfiche because I was trying to find out what happened with this guy I heard about on the radio, who killed somebody about ten years ago and recently got out of jail. Did you hear anything about that?"

"Was there something in the paper recently about this?" he asked.

"Yes, there might have been," I said. "I heard about it on the radio. The thing is, that same guy now lives next door to this kid I go to school with, and he used to know the kid's mom. And in fact, the kid's Dad was the guy that he killed. We found that out, me and Lucy and Lucy's mom, when we ran into Rev. Smith at the library. Rev. Smith, from my friend Mandy's church, you know, is the uncle of the guy who killed the kid's Dad."

"Well, I'm a little lost now. There's more going on in Possumtown than I thought," he said, thoughtfully, as he drove down the main road back toward the farm.

"The thing is, I think this guy might want to do something bad to this kid that I go to school with, or to his mother. He knew the kid's mother in high school, and he liked her, but she didn't like him. Mandy's Aunt Donna told us about that at church," I said, beginning to feel like I wasn't spelling it all out as clearly as I wanted to.

"So, you are worried about your school friend? What do you want me to do?" he finally asked.

"Could we just drop by his house, so I could tell him what I found out at the library? Please? It wouldn't take very long, he doesn't live that far, he's between where we live and the school."

"Can't you just tell him when you get to school on Monday?" asked Dad.

"I'm really worried about him, Dad. To tell you the truth, me and Lucy and her mom went by his house yesterday after we went to the library, and that man was talking to Rodney and Rodney looked scared."

"Rodney is this kid's name? He's a boy? Funny name. I didn't know you knew any boys," he said, not sounding like he was taking me seriously.

"Well, this kid is a boy, and he has younger brothers and a cute little sister, and I don't think their Mom is doing that much for them, they don't eat enough, and their clothes aren't clean. Just take me over there for five minutes?" I finished, almost in tears.

"I just think you're getting too worked up about this. I really don't think this kid is likely to have a problem, but if he does, his parents can deal with it, or else they can call the police. We are almost home, I didn't mind taking you to the library, but I am taking you home to dinner now, so your mother won't be upset with both of us. And please don't tell her about all this, the last thing we need is for her to decide that Possumtown is dangerous, for whatever silly reason, on top of all her other objections to living here."

I looked out the car window, and asked, trying not to cry, "Are we still going to move in a couple of months?"

"The plan right now," he said slowly, "is that your brother and I will be leaving at the end of this month, and you and your mother will follow us in a few more months when the school year is over."

"Remember you said we were going to stay here?" I said, my voice getting high and squeaky in spite of my effort to control it.

"Yes, of course," he sighed, "but I guess your mom and brothers don't like it here. I guess you and I are the only ones who do," and he patted my shoulder, but I moved away.

He went on, "I know you don't like the idea, but this opportunity for me to work in England won't come up again, and you might like it after you get used to it. You'll see. Anyway, you still have a few more months to be with your friends."

Well, so much for getting help from him. So, what could I do? What would a brave Middle Earth scout woman do? She would find a way to get the message through. I, however, couldn't think of a way to do it. I looked for Rodney's phone number and couldn't find it in the book. I dialed information and they gave me a number that turned out to be disconnected. I didn't think Mary would have Rodney's number yet, but I figured that I might as well call and ask.

"Lucy, did Rodney call your Mom, by any chance?" I asked her.

"What's up," she asked in a lilting tone, "did you want to call your lover boy?"

"Shut up," I said and told her what I'd seen at the library.

"Wow," she said, "I gotta admit, that does sound serious. Lemme ask Mom." She was gone for a minute, then came back.

"She didn't get any calls from him. She wanted to know if you looked in the phone book."

I said I did, and she told me to hang on. Then she was back, saying, "Okay, here's what she wants to do. Let's not worry about it tonight, what we can do is go over there a little earlier than we planned. Did you ask about your brother's clothes?"

"No, I forgot."

"Okay, do it in the morning. See if your parents can get you over here at ten. We can make the chicken then and bring it over at around noon, for lunch. You should see, it's a lot of chicken. And she found clothes for the babies and the little girl from an Avon customer of hers."

"Okay," I said, uncertain.

"That's really soon, Wilma," said Lucy. "I really don't think anything could happen between now and then."

I had to agree with her, until I watched that episode of the *Partridge family*, took the risky step of riding my bike out there, and found out that something could and did happen.

Chapter Seven

At Rodney's House

The question for me was, now that I was here at Rodney's house, in the middle of that Friday the thirteenth night, after that long bike ride, what could I do to help Rodney? Of course, I could help with the kids, but there was the bigger question of what to do about John Smith. That was something I didn't know, so it was just as well that the kids were a huge distraction.

Dan, the 10 year old brother, walked into the room just then, with his mouth full of peanut butter and crackers. "So, is Mom okay?" he wanted to know.

"She's okay," said Rodney, "just really tired."

"Do you want to give her some vodka again?" asked Dan.

Rodney looked at me, with that same half smile that was almost half shocked, and said, "We did that yesterday when she had a seizure."

"You gave her vodka?" I asked.

"Yeah, it's kind of a long story. Jeff told me about that, he said his Aunt Donna told him to do that when his mom had a seizure once. His mom drinks a lot too."

"And the vodka helped?" I asked, realizing this was probably the same Aunt Donna.

"Yeah, it did," said Rodney, with a little laugh, "I wasn't sure whether to believe it either, but it did help. And I would never have known what to do if I hadn't called Jeff. Good thing we have phone service right now, 'cause sometimes we don't, you know? It was scary, I gotta admit. I found her lying on the floor in the bathroom with her eyes shut and her arms and legs kind of moving around. I knew I should call an ambulance, but you know why I didn't want to. So, I called Jeff, and he told me what his Aunt said, to just pour some more booze into her. So, I did that, and she gradually stopped and finally sat up and was okay. Jeff said that she had the seizure from going without the booze for too long, so having more booze stops it. I couldn't understand how she wound up in the bathroom, but after she woke up, I walked her back to the couch and she told me she was looking for a bottle in there. You wouldn't think she could run out of booze with all these bottles around, but she said she couldn't remember where they were. When I told Jeff she was okay, he said, "I'm glad for you man, I would hate to see the authorities ship you off somewhere. Maybe these alky moms of ours are good for something after all."

He laughed a little. I didn't know whether to laugh or not. Finally, I said, "Well, it's amazing that you helped her like that."

"Yeah," he said, "she was better. So much better that she went out. I wish she didn't," he added, looking like he was about to remember that he'd just lost his mother. To change the subject, I decided to go out on a limb and ask him about the time I ran into him with Jeff the day before, when I dropped my book.

"So, when I saw you and Jeff on the stairs yesterday," I started, and he laughed.

"Oh, man, you were a little scary," he said. "You were grabbing at that book like it was a brick of gold."

I decided to ignore that. "Where were you guys going to eat lunch?"

"We just go up on the other side of the high school, where you can look down at Possumtown and Waggoner's Gap. We went camping there once, with the Scouts. We talk about going there again. That day we saw you, we were talking, I guess, about running track, and what we would do if we had money."

"What would you do?" I was curious.

"Well, get a car and get out of here, but I can't do that anytime soon on account of the babies. But it might be nice to have a few records and a record player. We only have a staticky little radio. I'd like some Beatles records, I think."

"My brothers have some," I ventured, "and sometimes I listen to them. They are good."

"Do you like the Osmonds?" he said with a snicker.

"No, well that is, I guess they're all right, but I don't have a crush on Donny. Some of the girls at school do. Don't bother asking, I am not going to tell you which ones."

"Do you have any records?" he asked, with a tone like, he could probably guess what they were.

"Okay, I have a few Neil Diamond records. You go ahead and laugh."

"Jeez. Well, that could be worse. I'm not sure how…"

"And sometimes I listen to my brother's Bob Dylan records. And I have one by Leonard Cohen," I said. "You heard of him?"

"No. I'm sure he's weird," he said, messing up my hair like I was his little brother.

Then he said to Dan, who was staring at us with a sort of grin that was almost laughing, "I don't think vodka would be good for Mom now. In fact, what would really help her out would be to get all her vodka bottles together and throw them out. She can't drink it anymore, and that way the babies won't find them and drink it by accident."

"Babies," I said, "what babies? I didn't see them when I was here with Mary and Lucy."

"Our youngest brothers are just babies still," said Rodney, "although the older one is walking and talking and acts like a little old man. They're sleeping right now."

"Oh," I said, "I would love to see them. When are they going to wake up?"

"Believe me, we don't want them to wake up right now. Best to leave them till morning, if they can sleep through all this. Sorry, but you just have to take my word on that," said Rodney, and then he asked Dan, "Do you know where any of the vodka bottles are? I know there's one under the chair cushion, and three in the bathroom."

"I think there's a few more in the babies' room, but they're sleeping," said Dan, "How about her box?"

"Her box?" I asked.

"Over there by the couch," said Rodney. They had a gray sofa and a matching overstuffed chair, somebody's leftover living room set from the 50s, and a coffee table with all the finish rubbed off. An old lamp with an egg-color shade covered with dust stood on a wooden box next to the sofa. On the wall was one photo of Rodney's mom with him and Dan, and on the fridge was a picture that Rodney made in art class of Nina, holding her two Barbies in either hand. Rodney saw me looking at this.

"You can really draw," I said.

He stopped for a minute and smiled, and told me, "When I made that and put that up, last fall, I told Nina that when the babies went to school and I get a job, I would buy her all the Barbie clothes she wanted. And she goes, 'Shoes too?' And I said, 'Of course the shoes. And pink ones, I know you like the pink ones.' And you know, she almost started crying."

"Wow," I said, and I wanted to hug him, but I just said, "You're a good brother. My brother would probably grab all my pink Barbie shoes and melt them for a science experiment."

Rodney laughed at this idea, then took a breath and said, "All right, let's look in the box first." Sure enough, a bottle was there underneath Miranda's clothes and things, a fifth, bigger than the other pint and half-pint-sized bottles. "Okay," said Rodney, "We'll pour this one out first."

He and Dan went to the kitchen where Nina was sitting, brushing the hair of her two Barbie dolls. One was an old one with a ponytail of blonde hair and sort of a smirking expression, wearing a black cocktail dress that had all the shine worn off of it, and the other was almost new and also blonde, with a gold and silver swimsuit. I sat next to her and we watched them pour the vodka into the sink. Then she looked at me quietly with her huge hazel eyes that looked just like Rodney's. "You really keep your Barbies' hair nice," I said, "I had one like her, with the ponytail, but I cut her hair short and she looked awful."

She giggled, then said, "I like to braid it, but I don't have rubber bands. So, I just braid them every day, and leave them like that."

"Do you guys have scissors?" I asked. She shrugged. I went to find Rodney. He and Dan were coming back to the kitchen, each with three or four vodka bottles.

"Whoa," I said, "Why did she keep so much vodka around? Would she have drunk all that?"

Rodney shot me a look, and Dan said, "She liked it a lot, but Rodney says she doesn't need it anymore. That's great, 'cause I don't like it. I think it makes her sick."

"Do you guys have a pair of scissors around here?" I asked.

"I don't think so," said Rodney, "what do you need them for?"

"To make something for Nina's Barbies. But we would need some cloth, too. An old towel or something."

He just looked at me, like, what now, but then he put the bottles down and left the room. It sounded like he was in the bathroom, and then he came back with a little, slightly rusty pair of nail scissors and a dried-out white washcloth with a brown stain on it. "Here you go," he said, and went back to pouring out the vodka.

Then Dan piped up again, "So why did Mom like to drink this so much?"

"Who knows?" responded Rodney. "She said something about her grandfather drinking once, but it didn't sound like he drank the way she does. It's way more than normal."

"I know," said Dan, "and it bothers me. She can't do much of anything with us, because she's drunk all the time. Chris' Mom takes them all over the place, they're always doing stuff like going to a movie or out to the mall in town. We don't even have a car."

"Well, that's going to change in a few years when I get my license," Rodney said, brightening up. Talking about driving and cars made him happy. "How about you Wilma, are you going to get a license when you turn sixteen? Everybody else around here does, there's no other way to get anywhere."

"I would like to, but to tell you the truth, there's no way to know where we will be living by that time. My parents are talking about moving again. I can't believe it," I said, shaking my head.

"What were they saying?" Rodney asked.

"Oh, nothing is for sure yet," I said, not wanting to talk about what my Dad said about moving to England. "I don't really like to think about it."

"Well, not living here could be a good thing for you. There's literally nothing to do," said Rodney. Then he had a thought.

"Dan, by the way, Mom was telling me something that I need to talk with you about. You know that you and me have the same Dad, right?"

"Uh huh."

"Not the same one as Nina and the babies."

"Of course," replied Dan, "I remember their dad, Daddy Ted. He only died last summer."

"Do you miss him?"

"Um. Yeah, I do. He was quiet, but he was nice to us, mostly," Dan said thoughtfully.

"You can't remember our Dad, because you were too little," said Rodney.

"Sometimes I think I can almost remember him a little bit," replied Dan.

"Probably not, little guy. You were just a baby. Truth is," said Rodney, "he used to yell at us when he was drunk."

"Really?" asked Dan.

"Yes. And hitting, sometimes. I was scared of him," said Rodney.

"Wow, that's awful," I said.

Rodney glanced at me, but then went back to talking to Dan. "So, you don't miss him?" asked Dan.

"No, not really."

"How old were you when he died?" I asked.

"Only about four. The thing is, she said something kind of important about the drinking," added Rodney.

"What was that?" asked Dan.

"She said, and she's probably right, that because he drank a lot, and he's our Dad, me and you need to make sure not to start drinking when we get older. Because we might wind up like him," Rodney finished, and looked Dan in the face.

He added, "Come here, Dan, and sit down with me at the table."

Dan sat, and wanted to know, "Hey, can we have some coffee?"

"I just want to make sure you heard what I just said. Look at me, okay? What did I just say about Dad's drinking?"

Dan frowned and stared at the table for a minute. Then he looked at Rodney and said, "That you and me can't drink booze because we might wind up being alkies like Mom and Dad."

Rodney laughed, "That's it, wow, you were listening to me. I never know, when you're moving around like that. She said that it was really important, and we have to remember it. Will you remember it, Dan?"

"Okay Rodney. But I really don't ever want to drink like Mom drinks."

"Me neither," said Rodney.

"Okay," said Dan, "can we have coffee now?"

"Yes," said Rodney, "we will have coffee. But there isn't much. Just one each."

"That's okay," said Dan.

"You can have milk in it, but you know we don't have sugar. Is that okay with you?"

"Sure," said Dan.

"Wow, your first cup of coffee," said Rodney with a smile.

"No," said Dan, quietly. "I had it at Chris's house once."

"Who is Chris?" I had to ask, hating to interrupt what seemed to be an important conversation. I was pondering how Rodney had double checked Dan's understanding of what he'd said, and how some of our teachers at the Junior High School could have learned something from that.

"Chris is Dan's friend who lives about a twenty-minute walk away, on the main road. He's a nice kid, and his mom is super nice, I guess. I never met her, and I ought to thank her some time for feeding Dan as much as she does. It helps us out a lot. You want some coffee too?" he asked me. I said yes, if there was enough, and he said sure. Then he asked Dan, "so what else happens at Chris's house that I don't know about?"

Rodney poured hot water on some instant coffee in three mugs, and handed them round to me, him and Dan. I only poured a little milk, since it seemed important to save it for Nina's cereal, and made a mental note to get them some sugar. Nina didn't want any coffee, but had a sip of mine, and then wrinkled up her nose and giggled. "We're going to make bathrobes for the Barbie dolls," I told her, "soon as I finish this," and she smiled.

Dan sat down at the ancient, chipped Formica table, put a generous amount of milk in his coffee, and stirred it thoughtfully. "Well, my favorite thing to do at Chris's house is to have peanut butter sandwiches, on bread, and chocolate milk. I mean, we have peanut butter, but theirs is better, and we never have chocolate milk."

"I had it that one time I went to Jeff's house," Rodney said. "Was it Nestlé's Quik, or Hershey's syrup?"

"Hershey's syrup"

"Yes," nodded Rodney approvingly, "that's the best. Well maybe one day we will have it here, but right now, with Mom sick like this, we need to save money even more than we already were."

Rodney took another sip of coffee and thought for a minute. Then he brightened up and added, "Come to think of it, Mom won't be needing that booze anymore. So maybe there is chocolate syrup in our future," he said, and ruffled Dan's hair.

"Quit it," said Dan, but not forcefully. He was thinking. Then he asked, "Why doesn't Mom need her booze? She always has. And we just threw it out, won't she be mad?"

"Oh," said Rodney, "well, the way she is right now, booze wouldn't be good at all. I mean it would just make her worse. In fact, you know what I'm thinking, is that we should make up a bed for her in the linen closet, so she can really have some peace and quiet."

"Really, there?" said Dan. "It's kind of small."

"Yeah, but quiet is what she needs most. We don't want the babies and the TV to disturb her. I can't think of anyplace else good except the attic, and she'll be too cold up there."

"Okay," said Dan. "What is she going to lie on? We don't have a bed that small, except for the baby cribs."

"I was thinking we could use the cushions from the sofa."

"Then what will we sit on?" Dan wanted to know.

"We don't need cushions," said Rodney. "We can just put a blanket or something on the sofa."

"Okay," Dan thought for a minute, then asked, "which blanket?"

Rodney said, "Mine, of course. I'll sleep out here now."

"Wow, you're not sleeping with us now? Too bad we can't use the extra bed for Mom."

"Yeah, but that room is too small. The bed won't fit," said Rodney.

"Wow", said Dan, "a whole extra bed. Could I have Chris over sometime?"

"Do you think he wants to come here?" asked Rodney, with a doubtful tone.

"He might. Maybe I'll ask him. Um, I don't know," Dan sighed, and then added, "he probably won't want to. Anyway, do you want help with Mom?"

"Wait a second," I said, "if you want help moving your mom, I think I should help you." I was worried that Dan might notice that his mom was dead and freak out.

"Don't worry," said Rodney, "Dan can help me. Come on Dan, let's put her on the chair for a minute while we move the cushions."

They picked her up, and her eyes rolled open, looking glassy and dark. Dan gasped. "Oh my God, what's wrong with Mom?"

I just stared. Poor Dan. Rodney quickly put her down and pushed her eyes shut again, then he put a towel over her face and said, "Nothing, it's okay. She's still sleeping. We don't want the light to bother her."

Dan stood and stared at Rodney for a minute, then shrugged and said, "I'll help you with the cushions."

"And I'll help with moving your Mom from now on. That's too hard for you, Dan," I said, not knowing how else to suggest that this child should not need to pick up his dead mother. We set the cushions in the little room, which was at the end of the hall between the babies' bedroom and the bathroom. The two bedrooms were on the left, and the bathroom and kitchen on the right side of the hall. I guessed that the babies were across from the bathroom because it helped with diapering, and I gave Rodney a lot of credit for dealing with that, since I myself had no real experience with it. He grasped his mother's shoulders again, being careful not to move the towel that he had placed over her head, and I somewhat gingerly picked up her ankles, and we carried her down the hall. Rodney set her on the sheet we had placed on the cushions, with a pillow under her lolling head, and almost cheerfully said, "There you go, Mom. Now you can have a nice rest."

Dan looked at him thoughtfully and said, "Do you think she needs a glass of water?"

"Oh no," said Rodney, "not right now. She needs to rest. I'm going to give her the couch blanket, and then I'll check on her again later. Good thing it's a Saturday. We won't be getting much sleep, will we? I think it must be at least two in the morning. The clock's in the kitchen, I'll check. Oh, it's two-thirty already. Do you want to call your parents, Wilma?" I looked at him, stunned. I hadn't thought about that even once. This being my first time out late at night on my own, it was also my first experience with that amnesia teens often get about calling their parents. I had to think for a few minutes.

Then I said, "I don't think so. I'm guessing they would've gone to bed, and if I call at this hour, they will get woken up and my mom will freak out. I'll call them in the morning and tell them I got up early and rode my bike to Lucy's house. They will believe it, 'cause I get up early a lot."

"Wow," said Rodney, "I guess you know how to handle them. Have you done this a lot, sneaking out at night to visit boys?" he asked, with a phony frown.

"No," I said, laughing, "first time."

Then I stopped laughing to think for a minute. "I did tell you about that guy's parents, right? I keep thinking I'm forgetting something important."

Rodney just looked at me, suddenly sad and tired. "Are you going to show us what you were doing about the Barbie dolls?" he asked, changing the subject.

We looked over at Nina at the kitchen table, who now had her head down, fast asleep. "We'll do it in the morning," I said, "where's her bed?"

"The front bedroom has a crib for her," said Rodney, "and two beds for me and Dan. I'll be sleeping on the sofa, though, so you can have my bed."

He picked Nina up, carefully, and took her into the bedroom. I noticed that only one of the other beds had a blanket. Watching Rodney put Nina to bed, I realized that the other blanket was on the couch for Rodney, and if I said something, he'd probably give it to me, and then he'd have a sofa with no cushions and no blanket or anything. So, for a change, I kept my thoughts to myself, and when he asked if I needed a blanket, I said, "No thanks, I can use my jacket. Hey, I'm just lucky you have a bed for me."

"Yes, you are," said Rodney, "because the floor smells like pee. I hope you don't mind Dan's snoring, his adenoids are huge, that's what makes him look like an overgrown chipmunk."

"I'll live," I said, laughing, and Dan looked embarrassed.

Then he said, with a sly look, "Rodney's just joking because he really wishes you were sleeping with him."

That really made me crack up, and I noticed Rodney was blushing, even though he was laughing too. He just said, "Go to bed, Dan."

And off we went to try to sleep what was left of the night. I reflected that at least it wasn't Friday the thirteenth anymore. Things couldn't get any worse. Maybe because it was so late, Dan was sleeping almost as soon as he put his head down, and indeed, he did snore like a little buzz saw. I lay there, still astounded by where I was and what had happened. Then I thought, *wait a second. Rodney's mother died tonight. How would I be feeling if that happened to me?* I couldn't sleep thinking about that, and it finally occurred to me that he probably wasn't sleeping either. Being careful not to wake the little ones, although I probably couldn't have anyway, I went out and looked in the living room.

Chapter Eight

Talking with Rodney

Rodney was sitting on the big chair, leaned over with his head in his hands. I sat down on one of the chair's arms. I didn't know what to say. After sitting there for a few minutes, I put my hand on his shoulder. He reached up and pulled me onto the chair next to him, almost in his lap. His face, wet with tears, was on my shoulder and he just held me and shook, sobbing quietly. Eventually the sobs were less frequent, and then they stopped. Without moving, he said, "You know, before you knocked on the door, I took a sip from one of those vodka bottles. It tasted awful, and I spit it out, but even so, I wonder if I would've started drinking it again if you hadn't shown up. I can't imagine what made you come over here, but I'm really glad you did."

I just sat there, in shock that I was sitting so close to him, and just drinking-in the feeling of that. He went on talking.

"Just the other day, after she had that seizure, my mom said, 'Too bad I love this stuff so much. I hope you never start drinking it.' And how my dad drank too much, and that meant that me and Dan could have drinking problems too. That's what I was telling Dan about."

"I thought it was really smart, the way you checked whether he was listening to what you were saying," I told him.

"Well, I have to do that with him sometimes, 'cause it can be hard to tell whether he gets what I'm saying. Anyway, I tried to cheer Mom up by turning on the radio, and it was that corny song, *Seasons in the Sun*. And believe it or not, we started talking about you. She said, 'I hope you get to have some 'seasons in the sun' one of these days. Don't any little girls have crushes on you?' and I said, 'there's one who stares at me a lot, but she's a little weird.'"

"Oh, huh," I said, "is that all you said, that I was 'a little weird?' I wonder."

He laughed and continued, "So Mom said, 'Hey, you're only in 8th grade. You don't know what these girls are going to look like in a few years. She might be really cute.'"

"Or," I said, "she might even be pretty cute now, and you just don't get it."

"Okay, calm down," said Rodney, laughing again. "Then she was talking about my dad. She always talked about him a lot. She said that in 8th grade, he was like a dwarf with an adenoid problem. But by graduation, he looked almost a foot taller and was playing football."

"Wow," I said, "he was a football player too. Oh, yeah." I stopped, not wanting to talk about what Rev. Smith said.

"Oh yeah, what?" asked Rodney. "Did you see something in that paper you were talking about?"

"Oh, no, not about that," I said, quickly. "What position did he play?"

"She said he was a fullback, which was good for him because he was a big guy, being six feet tall and broad chested, like Dan is going to be. Mom did right by giving him our Dad's name. Same mouth, too, and same crazy appetite. She said Dad was always stealing extra food from the cafeteria, just like Dan does now."

"Was your mom a cheerleader or something?"

"No, she never went in for that. She went in for parties, that was how they met. They both liked to drink too, of course. Dad was a little scary when he was drunk, but Mom always insisted that he loved us and was proud of me for being smart. He'd say, 'I guess Rodney takes after your side, Miranda, cause there's nobody that smart in my family.'"

"He was right about that, you are smart," I said, "I guess that's how you manage all the stuff you do. I couldn't do it."

"Who's really smart is GG, the bigger one of my baby brothers, he's almost two," said Rodney, "He's the one who acts like an old man, so smart and funny. I think he's going to be something special. He takes after his dad, Daddy Ted, who was my stepfather. Daddy Ted named GG after George Harrison, and Tom-tom after *Tommy* by the Who. And I think he loved my mom a lot. But sad to say, she didn't miss him all that much after he died. Maybe because he was quiet, and anyway he was high almost all the time. When she was drinking, she never mentioned Daddy Ted, but she'd say, 'I miss your Dad something fierce.'"

"Have you been doing everything by yourself?" I asked him.

"Most of it, since Daddy Ted died, last summer. Tom-tom was only a few months old when it happened, and GG is about a year older than he is. I used to help a lot anyway, so I knew what to do. I guess it's been over six months now that it's been like this. The only thing she did with me, lately, was to go to town to get her welfare check, and deal with the food stamps. I talked her into giving me most of the money, so we could pay at least some of the bills, and have money for food. I had to hide the money from her, or she would use it for booze. And the food stamps, too, 'cause she could give those to people to get booze. Sometimes she would even go out, and that was scary because I never knew what shape she's be in when she got back, or even whether she would make it back at all. And now this."

He shook his head slowly, biting his lip, and pulled me close again. I was so full of the feeling of being close to him, and yet sad for him, that I was almost delirious. But it felt right, somehow, to be with him like that. I almost felt like I could fall asleep that way, but not yet. I wanted to know more. "Tell me more about your mother. She was a beauty, right?"

"Yes, she was about the prettiest girl at the high school at the time, everybody says that, even though she didn't go in for cheerleading or any of that crap. She had those big hazel eyes, we all have them, and I guess it's the best thing she gave us, although none of us have eyes as beautiful as hers, except maybe Nina. She was like a model; thin, with high cheekbones and long eyelashes. She always used blue eyeshadow, trying to make that perfect line along the top of her eyes, but her hands shook, so she always put too much and smudged it."

"I've tried to do that, and I always smudge it too. It's hard," I complained.

"I can't imagine you with blue eyeshadow. Don't wear it to school, that's my advice. Nina likes to put it on her Barbie dolls, so funny."

"She is so cute with her Barbies, and she keeps their hair so nice," I said.

"Yes, she does," said Rodney, "too bad her own hair is such a dirty mess. Sorry to say, I only wash it once a week or so, and I just really don't know what to do after that. Mom used to braid it sometimes, but I never learned how. But Nina still looks pretty like Mom, and I look a little bit like Mom too. Dan looks just like our Dad, his and mine, the football player, with his mouth-breathing chipmunk face, but supposedly he'll get better looking. The little ones look a lot like Daddy Ted, especially GG."

"Why did she drink like that? Do you know?" I asked, with my head leaning against his, which was still on my shoulder. He spoke slowly, maybe a little bit sleepy finally, and what he had to say about his mother's life sounded almost like a dream.

"I asked her about this not that long ago. I remember my grandparents, they were really nice and such cute old people, you know? The Clampets, on *The Beverly Hillbillies*, kind of remind me of them. I'm pretty sure my mom's drinking drove them to an early grave, but I don't fully understand why she was so crazy about alcohol. The truth is, my mother didn't really understand it either, because she didn't remember the things that happened that probably led her to it, until her mother told her about something before she died. When my grandmother died, I guess I was six, so it's a while ago now. So, when she was dying, her sister, who was my mother's aunt, finally decided to talk about something that happened when my Mom was little, maybe two. Mom's father was going off to World War II, and her mother was devastated. He had enlisted at the start of the war, but wasn't accepted because he was too underweight, or something. However, by 1944 they were taking anyone they could to fight in the Bulge, and my mom's dad was one of them. The Bulge, that's what they were calling Belgium back then. I guess this was the last big battle of that war, but it lasted over a year."

"I think that's the same battle my Dad was in. Same thing, where he didn't get sent until the war was almost over, so he acts like it was no big deal, but I think he just doesn't want to talk about it."

"It's weird that my grandfather might have been close to the same age as your Dad," said Rodney.

"My Mom is younger than Dad, and she had a few miscarriages. I'm the youngest. That's why he was forty when I was born, and she was in her thirties."

"Wow. Anyway, so my grandmother took my mom, when she was about two, to stay with her parents and sister in Washington DC, and my grandmother's sister, who never married, was jealous and didn't like my mother, whose name is Miranda, by the way."

"Miranda, that's a beautiful name," I said.

"Yes," said Rodney "and she must have been a really cute little girl, like Nina is. Anyway, when my mom was a tiny girl, living there with her mother's family, they all began to sort of get the idea that the aunt didn't like her, but they just tried to ignore it and keep the baby away from her. But then came a week when her mother went to Atlantic City to see her husband's unit leave for Europe. While she was gone, my mom's grandparents let her Aunt take charge of bathing her, because they were too tired, I guess. And the Aunt took Mom to the basement to wash her in a tub with this special soap that stings a lot, I think they call it Naptha soap. The Aunt would soap her up, then dunk her under the water till she was almost drowning and laugh at her. Then she would take her out, crying, and give her a slap in the face to make her stop. She dried her off, put her clothes on and braided her hair, and warned her not to say anything unless she wanted more slaps. When Mom told me about it, she said she had never even remembered it until her mom was telling her what her Aunt had said, and then something came back to her. And listen to this…she had dreams throughout her whole life where some powerful big hand was pushing her under water and laughing. And she said that sometimes, when she was really drunk, she would feel that hand on her again and she would think, *Now go ahead and do your worst, because I don't care. In fact, I like the feeling of drowning, so you can't make me cry anymore.*

"Wow," I said, "That is so sad. Do you think that happens a lot, where people don't remember things that happen when they're really little, and then they wind up dreaming about it, or something else happens that reminds them about it? My Dad told me once that I got freaked out when I was a baby and my mom accidentally let the car crash through the garage door, and after that I would go into a panic whenever they drove through a covered bridge."

"Where are there covered bridges? I don't think we have any around here."

"I guess there used to be a few back in Ohio. I barely remember going through any, but that's what he said," I shrugged.

He lifted up his head and stretched a little. "Do you want a glass of water or something?" he asked me.

"No, I'm okay. You know, I met Mandy's Aunt Donna at the church a few weeks ago, and she said she had a friend in high school named Miranda. Was that your mom?"

"Yes, that would have been her. Donna tries to call us once in a while, but Mom never wanted to talk to her because she didn't want her to know that she had been drinking. But we saw her at Daddy Ted's funeral last summer. She's always really nice to us."

"That's good," I said, "she did seem like a nice lady. Anyway, I want to know what it was like for you. Did she used to be drunk here all the time, and you would be here with her?"

"I guess I got kind of used to it. Watching her drink, and talk, and listen to music and smoke cigarettes. It made me feel sad, but I loved to watch her anyway. You know, it was like, she didn't want her real life, she wanted some pretend life that she got from the drinking. When she was drunk, well, I think she pretended that my dad was still alive. Sometimes she listened to music and it almost seemed like she thought she was talking to him or dancing with him even, at a party or something. Her eyes would light up when she did that, but it was so sad, because Tom-Tom or GG or even Nina could be doing something really cute, or talking to her, and she wouldn't even notice."

I looked at Rodney and said, "Wow, it's like she couldn't have the life she wanted, so she was not really living the life she had."

He looked back and said, "Yeah, kind of like that."

Chapter Nine

The Ponytail Guy

"So how did she know the guy with the ponytail?" I asked Rodney, adding, "I wonder why they were fighting."

"I don't know much about him. I only met him because he took some money from us."

"He broke into the house?"

"No," said Rodney, looking uncomfortable. "This was kind of dumb, but I was worried Mom would find the money I was hiding in the house, so I took part of it and hid it outside. I dug a hole next to the tree and put a big rock over it. I guess that seemed kind of obvious. Anyway, when I came back from school a few days ago, most of the money was gone."

"What did you do?" I asked.

"Well, first I went and asked John Smith about it. That was the first time I spoke with him."

"Wow, you are brave. I don't think I could have done that," I said.

"Don't think I enjoyed it. I hate talking to strangers, or almost any adults besides my Mom, really. And I remembered what Mom said about this man being mean to everybody in high school, but I just couldn't think of any other way to find out. So, I went over there. I was so nervous, I just barely knocked on the screen door, and he yelled at first, but then he got all nice and friendly when he saw who I was. He offered me a Coke, and I said I didn't want one, but he got me to sit with him and gave me a Coke anyway. His furniture is new, it looks so different than ours. The wood is so smooth. Anyway, he said he saw a blond guy with a pony tail looking around our house, peeking in the windows, and then he went in the back. And he said, never hide stuff in your yard, and it's really obvious if you put a rock on it. He wanted to know if the guy was looking for my mother, and I said I didn't know. Then I saw he had a big whiskey bottle on the kitchen counter and a rifle in the corner of the room, so I told him I had to get back to the house and got out of there as fast as I could."

"Wow, that is scary," I said, "I don't know if I've ever seen a rifle close up."

"So, then I saw the guy with the ponytail down the road when I was on my way back to the house. I asked him who he was, and he said his name was Jerry, that he was looking for my mother, and he said sorry about taking the money. I told him that we really needed that money back, with two babies to feed, because formula and diapers cost a lot. He asked me how old the babies were, and I said ten months and nineteen months, and he wanted to know if we were Catholic."

"Ha," I said, "That is what people used to say in Dayton whenever somebody had a big family."

"Nothing wrong with being Catholic, but it's still a rude thing to say. Then he went on and said, 'You need to get those babies off formula.' Like it was his business. But still, it kind of got to me and I started thinking about it."

"It might be a good idea. That formula does cost a lot, right?" I was guessing.

"Yes, it is a good idea, but he was still being rude, and I was getting mad. He says, 'What's going on with your mother? Is she just drunk or passed out all the time? How does she stay alive like that?' And I said, that it really wasn't his business and I just needed my money back."

"Good for you," I said, "Rodney, you really know how to talk to grown-ups. I don't think I could have said that, but it is the truth, that's for sure."

"He ripped me off, first of all, and then he was rude. But here is the big surprise: he gave the money back."

"Wow," I said, "that's amazing. I wonder why he bothered to take it in the first place?"

"Well, I started wondering, too," said Rodney. "He asked me if I would let him talk to my Mom if he gave me the money, and I said no, but he gave it to me anyway, most of it. It was weird, really. I think he probably took it just to have an excuse to talk to us."

"Was he a friend of your Mom's?"

"I don't think he knew her that well. I really don't know why he would have hurt her, except he must have been drunk or something. She said something the other day about somebody wanting her to help them sell pills. Maybe that was what they were arguing about."

He stretched again, and asked, "So, what about this moving thing? Is that really going to happen?"

I frowned and looked away. He laughed. "Uh-oh. I'm sitting here spilling my guts, and you still don't want to talk about that? Come on, I'd like to know. I'm beginning to think it would be nice to have you around for a while."

I looked back, and I was almost scared to see him looking at me like this was really important to him. I wasn't sure anybody had ever looked at me like that before. It felt scary in a good way. I wasn't able to meet his gaze for very long though, I guess it felt like too much, so I looked away, and the next thing I knew, he was kissing me. That felt a little bit like drowning, putting me in mind of what happened to Rodney's mother. Maybe it could feel sort of good to drown for a little while. When we stopped kissing, I was just unable to think anymore, so I sort of buried my face in his chest. I thought I was going to cry and spent a while sitting like that and wondering if I was going to start crying, but I didn't. Finally, I looked up at him again.

"So," he said, "this is where we don't move over to the sofa. Because you're probably not ready for that, and anyway you might be moving, so it wouldn't be good to get too crazy here."

I had to smile at this. Then I giggled over a thought that came to me. "You know," I said, "you kind of remind me of Aragorn."

"Ara what? Who the hell is that, some TV person I never heard of?" He was laughing too. Finally, he leaned forward and got up.

"I hate to get up, but I was starting to get a cramp in my leg. That happens every time I fall asleep on that chair. Which I have been doing a lot of, recently. You want a drink of water now? I do, so I'll get you one too."

He went to the kitchen. I got up too, and stretched. It was the same world, but it seemed different. Warmer. I giggled again, thinking about what I'd said to Rodney. If Aragorn hadn't met Arwen, would he have been interested in some average chick like me? Probably not, but Rodney seemed to be, and I thought he was just as cool. Certainly, he was about as brave as Aragorn, dealing with that scary John Smith guy. He came back with the glass of water.

"What were you giggling about," he asked, "that guy again, Aragorn? Nina watches TV all the time, of course, but I guess the rest of us just watch reruns of

The Beverly Hillbillies, and some cartoons, besides *The Partridge Family*."

"Oh, that's a book character. He's not on TV. I watch *The Partridge Family* too. Last night they had that episode about the Mother of the Year. That's the reason I felt like I had to come out here, because I couldn't stand the idea that the weird guy might wind up poisoning your mother. Oh, I'm sorry, I didn't want to make you sad again."

He was suddenly looking thoughtful and staring at his glass of water as if he could read his future in there. I went to hug him, but the glass of water was in the way, so I put my hand on his shoulder again. Eventually he said, "I keep forgetting that everything is different now. Just one night, and the whole world changes."

I frowned, thinking of how happy I had felt a few moments ago, and it seemed selfish to me now, like I was forgetting how much pain Rodney must be feeling. I wished I knew what to say. I just kept my hand there, and waited until I might get an idea, but it never came. I closed my eyes, and in my mind, I saw a picture of the sun rising behind the creek, and the birds beginning to sing. I looked at him again and said, "When people die, they often say that at least the person is at peace, and their pain is over. Maybe your mother is in a good place now. I don't know if it helps you to think about that. I can't think of anything else. I'm not really good at this, I guess."

He put down the glass of water, hugged me, and said, "Just that you're here is so amazing. You really came here because you thought we were going to get poisoned by that guy? You know, most people would have just shrugged and said 'Hey, too bad,' and gone to bed or something."

He kissed me, and I was in that place of sweet drowning again.

Then he looked at me and said, "Of course, this wasn't part of my plan. I hope I didn't hurt your feelings, but I honestly thought you were kind of a weirdo. I didn't want a girlfriend anyway, because the whole idea kind of scares me. But now, I guess I would feel kind of bad if you weren't going to be my girlfriend. So, we have to figure out how to get you out of moving away. Maybe I could let the air out of your dad's tires, or something."

I laughed, "That wouldn't work for very long."

He said, "It would if I did it every day. I could sneak over there. Maybe you could let me use your bike. But we can't do anything too crazy. I don't want you to be talked about all over school, like that girl who was in the car with Mike Brecht too long. And I don't want you talking to Mike Brecht, either, come to think of it."

"Don't worry, he never talks to me or even looks at me or any of my friends. We would know. Or at least Lucy would. But I guess I'm lucky you know what to do about that. I don't think I would hold out long."

"Hmm. Maybe you shouldn't have told me that," he said, and kissed me again. Then he looked me right in the eyes and said, "Don't worry, though. We're going to do this right. I don't want you to get in trouble for coming out here to help me."

I leaned my head against his chest, and thought I was going to pass out again, but I didn't, and then for some reason I started to giggle. "That would be a problem," I said, "especially if Lucy's mom found out. She gave Lucy a long talking-to about that very subject, in front of me, and I know she said it in front of me for a reason. Plus, she talks to everybody. People we never heard of would be talking about us."

He laughed, and said, "And more important than that, if we even figured out what to do, which I'm not sure if I could but maybe, then there would be a baby down the road. That is what Mr. Snagidag said in Health class, right? And you know I couldn't deal with any more babies."

The thought of our nice old Health teacher made me laugh so hard I had to sit down. "Can you imagine him if I got pregnant? What would he say in his class after that?"

"He'd tell them not to act like us. Don't go making babies like Rodney and Wilma, he'd say. Your mother getting killed is no excuse." Then he stopped laughing and sat down next to me and put his head in his hands again. He sat like that for a while, and I put my arms around him and waited until he was ready to talk.

"I just don't know what to do tomorrow. Do I call the police or not?"

"I think it would be a good idea, because they could help you with that guy," I said.

"But what would they do with the kids? Would they put them in homes?" he asked.

"I don't know," I said, "but Lucy's mom wants to come during the day and bring you guys some food and spare clothing. Do you think you could talk with her about it?"

"Oh, man, she's coming here? When was she going to come?" He almost got up, looking at me with a shocked expression.

"Maybe lunchtime?" I said, not remembering too well all of a sudden.

"Can you call her and tell her not to come? After you call your parents?"

"But why not let her bring the food? You guys are hungry, I can tell you're not eating enough. And her cooking is the best, I can tell you."

I really wanted them to have some of Mary's fried chicken. "But think, Wilma," said Rodney, still looking horrified as he went on, "this isn't a book. Okay, I'm sorry I said that," he added, probably noticing that I was getting mad, "but listen, my mom's body isn't going to be a secret forever. Sooner or later she's going to start to smell bad. People are going to be able to tell."

"Look, I'm not crazy like my brother. I know it's not a book," I said, not even sure why it made me so mad that he said that.

"I know you're not. But this is a crazy situation. Neither of us knows what to do. We have to figure it out. I know I have to tell people that Mom's dead sooner or later. But just not right now, okay?"

"Okay," I said, "You're right, and I keep forgetting that your mother is in that room. I wish I knew what to do about it. We can't just haul off and bury her, though. That guy would see us."

"No, and anyway, I don't want him to know she's dead, yet. He might try to do something then. I just need time to think. Do you want to try to sleep? I don't think I can, but let's lie down on the couch, and you see if you can sleep a little."

So, we did that, and I forgot right away that he had more or less told me I was crazy. It felt great to be lying down next to him like that, and he made another joke about not wanting to be like those two kids in the car who got carried away and all.

Chapter Ten

Cereal is Neato

I must have fallen asleep, because the next thing I remember is waking up and hearing young voices I hadn't heard before. It took me a few seconds to remember where I was, and then Rodney came walking in the room with a baby in his arms and another little boy, walking but still small, right next to him. He said, "Good morning, and I hope you're ready to meet these guys 'cause they've been crazy to meet you. It was all I could do to keep GG from waking you up. This is him," pulling the little boy forward. He was a serious little thing with very full cheeks, big hazel eyes like all of them had, and a fuzz of blond curly hair around his head like a halo. He said, "Hi! Who you?"

"I'm Wilma," I said, "Are you GG?"

"Yis," said the boy, "Gonna eat. Cereal. Come."

"He wants you to come to the kitchen and watch him eat cereal for the first time. Remember I told you about that guy who was with my mom, how he took that money? And I was talking about how much their formula cost, and he told me that I should get them on solid food. Not like I really know what I'm doing, but I asked GG if he wants to try cereal, and he does."

"So, GG is short for George?" I asked.

"That's how Nina said his name, and it kind of stuck."

"That's really cool," I said, looking in awe at the two of them. The younger one was bald, but with the same big eyes and cheeks, except the cheeks might have been even bigger, if that were possible. Both were placid and seemed just thrilled to be there.

"Are they always this wonderful?" I had to ask.

"No," said Rodney.

We went to the kitchen and he handed me the little one. "He can hold his own bottle, but he likes to sit in people's laps. It's your turn."

"Great," I said, smiling at the cute little soul and smelling milk and baby sweat on his head, which was directly under my nose. It was a new smell to me, and I loved it.

Before Rodney got the cereal out, Dan came in the room. He looked at me. "You didn't sleep in the bed?"

"I couldn't sleep," I told him, and looked at Rodney, who smiled and said, "What's it to you, nosy?"

Dan looked at both of us and said, "Uh huh. Well, anyway. I hope you guys didn't eat all the cereal."

"We wouldn't do that," said Rodney, laughing, and turned to me and said, "Dan thinks with his stomach. Okay Dan, here's the cereal. Have as much as you want, we can get more later."

"Won't the milk run out?" Dan wanted to know.

"Well, save some for Nina. Wilma and I can eat it dry. I got some formula for the babies, but we need more. Like I said, we're going to the store later. And give me the milk first, before you pour it. I want GG to try some cereal."

"Okay, wow, GG, your first cereal," said Dan.

"Wow," said GG.

"How come you all of a sudden decided to give him cereal?" Dan asked Rodney.

"Some friend of Mom's said something about it," said Rodney, not blinking.

"You know who else would know about that? Chris' mom. Can we go there after the store? Maybe you could talk to her for a minute," said Dan.

"Wow, Dan," said Rodney, "that is actually a really good idea. I think we should do that."

"Just don't stick around too long," said Dan, with a look of concern.

Rodney laughed, "Okay, Dan, we won't mess up your special deal with Chris and his mom, who feeds you all the time. We need her to keep doing that. Speaking of feeding," he took a spoon with a couple of pieces of cereal on it and popped it in GG's mouth. GG's eyes went wide, and he pursed his lips, his cheeks sucked in while he explored this new food item with his tongue.

Dan collapsed with laughter, "He's freaking out. Look at his face. GG, are you okay?"

GG frowned and said, "GG 'kay. Cereal good."

He continued to move his tongue around his mouth cautiously. Dan was still laughing, and said, "he doesn't know how to chew. It's a riot."

GG frowned again. "Does chew. GG does. Can. Want more. More cereal."

Rodney smiled and handed him the spoon. "Can you hold it?"

"Sure," said GG. "Neato."

I gasped, "GG, that's great. Rodney, where did he get 'neato' from? So cute."

GG looked at me with some concern, but Rodney said, "It's okay, GG. Just pay attention to how you're holding the spoon and try not to spill it. That's good."

Then he turned to me and said, "GG got most of his words from us kids, I think, but once in a while he comes out with something Mom used to say, and neato is one of those. She used to spend more time with the babies, but like I said, she kind of stopped when my stepfather died. My stepfather used to play with them too, but at some point, he just stopped doing pretty much everything."

"Wow," I said, "that's so sad. I can't imagine how he wouldn't want to spend time with these adorable babies."

"Well," said Rodney, "they're having a good day, and they're good babies but sometimes they can be pretty tough going. But he loved them a lot, so it did seem kind of strange. I don't know if it was the drugs, or just being sad, or what. I mean, he and Mom were so happy at first, and I thought it was great that Ted was nice to us and didn't yell at us like my Dad did. But somehow things kind of went bad, especially when the little guys came. I mean, Nina was different, she was such a beautiful little girl, just like a little angel from day one. But later on, after she had GG, Mom began to change. She would get mad at all of us for no reason, and yell at Ted, poor guy. And he would just listen and nod his head, and roll another joint. I was hoping things would get better when the babies got bigger, but she just got worse all the time, and then suddenly Ted just died. I know he tried stronger drugs sometimes, so it was probably an overdose, and I can't help wondering if he did it on purpose. But I guess we'll never know."

"I'm sorry," I said, "he sounds like a nice man. And he was GG and Tom-tom's father. Nina was his child too? And then you and Dan.."

"The football player. You're getting it, all right. Yes, me and Dan had a different father than Nina, GG and Tom-tom. Their father was Daddy Ted."

"You said Daddy Ted died last summer?"

"July, I think. I don't even remember much about the funeral, just a gathering of us and a few of my Mom's friends. She stopped nursing Tom-tom right after that. I wound up doing almost everything, and sometimes it seemed like they forgot about Mom. They looked for me to change and feed them. It helped a lot that they were good babies."

"They sure are," I said, "but it's still amazing to me that you know how to take care of them. I wouldn't have any idea."

"Well, they are good, most of the time, and they usually don't cry unless they have a good reason. Tom-tom had a touch of colic around the time his Dad died, and he cried almost all the time for a week or so, but finally he calmed down. It may have helped that GG began looking out for Tom-tom, he's so funny, you will go nuts when you hear him, and sooner or later he's bound to start. He goes, "Roddy, come. Tom-tom pee. Tom-tom seepy," or whatever it is."

I smiled and looked at GG. "He's like you, he just knows how to take care of things."

GG looked up at me in mid-spoon, kind of nonchalantly, as if to say, "Of course."

"He really is a smart little guy", said Rodney, "and he stopped crying almost completely when he was only eight or nine months old. It was like, he figured out that the crying didn't work, and that nothing much would happen unless I was around, and then he just called me, 'Roddy.' He learned my name before 'Mama,' or just about anything else."

GG had managed to get the spoon to his mouth, get some cereal in there and put it back in the bowl. He picked the spoon up again, but a little too fast, and it wobbled. "Uh-oh."

"It's okay," said Rodney, over Dan's howls of laughter. "You can sit closer to the table. That way if you drop it again, it won't go on the floor. You're doing just great."

"Oh boy," chortled Dan, as Rodney pushed him back to the living room. "That was something to see, alright."

"Why don't you watch some cartoons?" said Rodney, "Aren't *the Banana Splits* on? Don't you like them?"

"Yeah," said Dan, "but they're not on till nine, it's just *the Pink Panther* now."

Chapter Eleven

Calling Home

Dan and Rodney both froze at the knock on the door. It was John Smith again. Rodney went back to the kitchen and told me, "Keep the kids in the kitchen while I talk to him and don't open the door." He turned to the kids and said, "Okay you guys, go have some more cereal with Wilma while I see what this guy wants. Then we can go to the store." When we were all in the kitchen with the door shut, he reluctantly opened the front door.

"I don't like that man," Dan told me. GG looked a little worried.

"Roddy?" he said to me.

"He's all right," I smiled at this impossibly cute little boy. "Show me again how you eat the cereal. You really learned that fast," I said, and he smiled proudly. I had been holding Tom-tom, and sat down with him in my lap. He grinned and did one of his cute noises, "Bee-bee."

It was so nice sitting there next to GG with Tom-tom in my lap, watching GG make his funny faces with the cereal in his mouth, that I almost forgot about the scary neighbor. But then Dan opened the door an inch or two so he could listen, and filled me in.

"He's saying something about how his wife is coming."

"John Smith has a wife? I wonder.." Then I stopped talking, thinking that Dan didn't need to hear me talking about his mother.

But Dan may have figured out what I was about to say, telling me, "Rodney told me that he used to know my Mom."

"Really, wow," I said, not wanting to mention that my friend's aunt had already told me that. Did he know Aunt Donna, I wondered and asked, "Does your mom have other friends? Like, people that she used to know when she was in school?"

After thinking for a minute, Dan said, "One lady calls her sometimes. Her name is Donna. And I think there's another one, but I'm not sure."

Maybe Jeff's mom, I was thinking. Is that why Jeff and Rodney were close, or did it just wind up that way? "Is that man leaving yet?" I asked Dan. He listened.

"Yeah, now he is," he said, looking at me, relaxed and happy again.

Rodney came in the room and said, "Okay, let's get ready to go, everybody. Wilma, come with us to the store, okay? You want to call your mom first?" Saying that, he suddenly stopped short and looked bereft again. All the kids were staring at him. He forced himself to smile. "Dan, show Wilma where the phone is."

"Is that guy okay?" Dan asked Rodney.

"I guess," Rodney replied. "I think maybe he used to know Mom, but we don't really know him. He's only been there a short time." He suddenly looked tired, and said, "You know, let's have the rest of that coffee. I can buy some more. We'll make that, and we can drink it while we're getting ready to go and Wilma's using the phone."

"Oh boy," said Dan. "Great."

Then he showed me where the phone was, next to the couch on that box that used to have the fifth of vodka in it. Suddenly Dan had tears in his eyes.

I didn't know if he would want me to hug him yet, so I said, "She'll be okay," and patted his shoulder.

He suddenly hugged me, tightly, his body contracted as if he were about to sob, but he didn't. Instead, he nodded, blinked back his tears, and said, "Yes, Rodney's taking care of her." Then suddenly I realized, he knew. This brave kid knew his mother was dead and wasn't saying anything. I put my arm around his shoulder, but I didn't know how to ask him about it. Just then from the TV came *the Banana Splits* theme song.

"You like this show?" I asked him, "you want to sit and watch it with me for a minute?"

He nodded, "Sure."

So, we both sat on the couch and pretended to watch, him blinking back tears and me thinking how brave he was, and whether I could do something more to help Rodney and these kids. Then I remembered I had to call home. So, I did, and Gil picked up the phone. "What?" he laughed, "aren't you in bed?"

I said, "I got up early and rode my bike to Lucy's house. Where's Mom and Dad?"

"They're still in bed," he said, "Jeez, if it was any other girl your age, you'd be at some boy's house. But since it's you and we all know that you don't know any boys, then I don't think Mom's really going to worry that much," he said, still laughing.

"Well, good," I said, kind of mad, but I wasn't sure why. "Isn't that the important thing, not to upset Mom? Anyway, you just tell them I'm at Lucy's house."

"Okay, got it, Wilma," he said in a mock serious tone, laughing even harder, and I hung up. I must have looked mad, because when Rodney saw me, he looked curious.

"What did they say?" he asked.

"It was Gil, my brother," I said, "he said he believes me, because I don't know any boys."

Rodney looked at me and laughed. Then he came over and put his arms around me for a second, and said, "Well, do you know any boys, Wilma?"

"I wish I could tell him. I'd love to see what he looked like when he found out."

"Might be for the best if that doesn't happen today," Rodney laughed again, "but when it does, I'd love to have a front-row seat," he added, and then went to get me some of that coffee.

Then we all went out to the couch and sat with Dan, the three of us with our coffee, Nina with her cereal, and the babies just wandering around looking cute. When we finished the coffee, and Nina ate all her cereal, they got their sweatshirts on, to go to the store. I picked up my jacket. "Aren't we going to say bye to Mom?" asked Dan.

"Oh, right. I'll check on her," said Rodney.

"Let me come with you," I said.

Rodney looked into the room, brightly said "Okay, Mom?" Then he went inside, letting me in and shutting the door behind us.

"Do you think she's starting to smell bad?" he asked me.

"Yeah, I do notice something. Sort of a rotten-egg smell. I wonder if we could do something about that."

"She doesn't have any perfume. I looked," said Rodney. "Is there anything else that would help?"

"Maybe baking soda? We use that in the laundry sometimes. We could get a whole bunch, it's really cheap, and sprinkle it on her. It might help," I said.

"Okay," said Rodney.

And he carefully pulled the towel over her face again, making sure not to look too hard. Then he went to the kids and they trooped out.

"I'm locking the door this time," said Rodney. "Now if you get locked out, Dan, you know which window is always open, don't you?"

"Our bedroom window," said Dan.

"That's right. And remind me to get some baking soda."

"For what? Are you going to bake something?" asked Nina, suddenly excited.

Rodney smiled, "Oh, no little girl, it's just for something Wilma and I are going to do. Did you guys get your sweatshirts? I'll get the babies theirs, and I'll get money too. Nobody look, now."

Dan looked at me, grinned and said, "He hides it from us, and we're not allowed to look. So, Mom won't find out and take some."

"So why hide it from you?" I wondered.

"We would tell her," he said, without hesitation.

I had to laugh, "Well, at least you're honest about it."

Rodney had two strollers, a nice one for the babies, built for two, that somebody gave his mom after Tom-tom was born last summer, that was still in good shape, and another, older one that was pink and cute-looking but dragged a bit. There was another totally broken one from when Rodney and Dan were little, but that was just for Nina to play with in the yard. When we went outside, I looked around a little, since I only got one look at the house in daylight, back with Mary and Lucy, and that was too brief to really notice anything much. I was curious about the yard and went with Rodney and Nina to fetch a forgotten piece of doll furniture that she wanted for her Barbies. Dan held on to the babies' stroller for me. He was thrilled not to have to push them to the store, as he normally would.

The house was a small bungalow style with scrubby grass in front and a backyard full of weeds, broken toys, and empty bottles. There was a small tower out of the old vodka bottles that shone in the morning sun. "Who made that?" I asked.

"Dan," said Nina, then added, "for a while we had a fort. Dan made it out of a big cardboard box. I used to play house with my Barbies, but the wind blew it away. I almost lost my Barbies. Rodney had to look all over for them," she added, looking at Rodney with her eyes big.

Rodney laughed, "Yes I did. Whenever the weather gets bad, I have to run outside and do a toy check, or the Barbies might be gone forever. That time, they were all the way in the weeds, almost in the neighbor's yard."

"I used to have Barbies, and I still have most of my stuffed animals. I should show you sometime,

Nina. But what I really used to like was books, and I still do. Do you guys ever have books around?"

"I did notice that you liked books, Miss Wilma," Rodney said, laughing again. "You like them a little too much. That big book you carry around looks like it weighs a ton. Do you actually read it, or you just carry it around so you can talk about it with Mrs. Strough?"

"Did I hear you talking with Jeff about that, making fun of me? You made it sound like I was like that lady on *Laugh-In*, going "ahem" all the time. I do not do that."

Rodney, still laughing, said, "but you do, sometimes. What is it, do you always have a cold? You're always with the tissues and clearing your throat all the time, and you wind up sounding exactly like that."

"Well, too bad about that, I have allergies, so what?" I said, again kind of mad. Or maybe I was really mad. Truthfully, I still pretty much only ever get "kind of" mad.

"What are you allergic to?" he asked, wiping his eyes a little. Apparently, my allergies were a real riot.

"I get hay fever, okay? It isn't that funny to me. Right now, I'm okay, but in September I will be all messed up again. I hate it," I said, and that was the truth.

It still is. Nina looked up at me. "Wilma, you okay?" she asked, all concerned.

"Oh of course I am, Nina," I said, picking her up. "I can't wait to go to the store with you. Rodney, can we get these kids some cookies?"

"Cookies," said Nina, looking like she received a sudden jolt of electricity.

"We'll see," said Rodney, looking at me like, shut up already.

"Do you ever look at books, Nina?" I asked.

"Sure," she said, "GG has *Pat the Bunny*."

I laughed. "Well, that sounds like a good place to start."

Rodney said, "Once in a while a teacher gives me or Dan some books, but we don't do much reading. I'm not even sure Dan knows how to read, and I don't really have time to show him, but he doesn't seem to worry about it. He spends most of his time after school playing ball or watching TV with some of his friends who live up by the main road. And with any luck, the friend's mom would invite him for dinner, and he wouldn't come home to eat a whole can of soup and most of the crackers himself. He's hungry all the time, I swear. Nina watches TV all the time, just about. And plays with her Barbies, of course," he said, smiling at her.

"Do they help with the babies?" I wondered.

"I don't bother them about that," said Rodney, "unless Dan is around to help us get to the store. But I figured they probably needed a break."

"And do you ever get a break?" I had to ask.

"Not since Tom-tom came along," he said, with one of his half smiles. "But I got ideas for the future. When I can get a job, and the babies are in school, I will get a car, and everything will change."

"I wish we had that car now. Seems like a long way to push these strollers," I couldn't help saying. He shot me a look. "Not that I mind," I said quickly, "but you have to do this almost every day, don't you?"

"Yep," he said, "and that's why I really want to get a car as soon as I am able to. Can't wait."

Chapter Twelve

Going to the Store

We got the strollers in front of the house, and Nina got into her pink one, that must have been bought for her when she was a baby, with her Barbies and a little pink blanket, looking very cute and comfortable. I wanted to push her, but Rodney said the stroller got stuck sometimes and he didn't want me to have to deal with that. He gave me the good stroller and put the babies in it for me. GG got in under some protest, since he wanted to walk at first, but Rodney insisted that it was too far, and he could walk when they got to the house of Dan's friend, Chris. That kept him quiet, since I guess he was excited about visiting someone else's house for a change. Nina, on the other hand, was happy to get into hers. Rodney told me quietly that she walked to the store sometimes with him, if Dan was busy at his friend's house, but had to take turns with GG on the way back because it was still a little too far for her.

It was a nice sunny morning, though a bit chilly. The road was lined with trees that filtered the golden light of the morning sun. Spring in Possumtown just seemed springier; there was a green quality to the light and the air. Not just the trees and the flowers, but the bees and other insects were whirring with life by this time of the morning. I liked to imagine that it was like the forest of the Ents, one of my favorite parts of *The Lord of the Rings*. Well, so much for that, except that I couldn't imagine any hobbit, elf or human children more appealing than these little ones here, and of course I needed to talk with Nina about her Barbies.

"The one with the ponytail is Miranda, like Mommy," she said, "Mommy got her for me when we went to the flea market. The other one is just Barbie; Mommy's friend gave her to me after Daddy Ted left us."

It felt weird to hear her refer to her dead father, when she was so tiny. She was little for four years old, looking like a slim and precocious toddler, but sometimes coming out with these statements that showed she was older than she looked. "Nina is such a pretty name," I told her, and she smiled.

Rodney said, "My mom named her that, because of that famous cartoonist that put his daughter's name, Nina, in all of his drawings of famous people, that you see in the papers sometimes. So that she would feel more special, I guess. Mom used to say that she wanted her to remember that we love her, just like that other girl whose father put her name in all those cartoons. I never understood why that made it a good idea, but it is a pretty name. Truth is, she and Daddy Ted were both getting high a lot."

"So, you go to the store like this almost every day, right? How come you don't get more stuff and just go once a week, is that because you can't carry it all?" I had to ask.

"Well that's part of it, but the other part is, if I buy a lot of stuff, my Mom will try to trade it for booze sometimes. Either take it back to the store, or just get money for it. So, I learned not to get too much at once. The only thing I buy in bulk is the diapers. For some reason, she never takes those back. And people might want them. But I guess that's her way of taking care of the babies, just to leave their things alone. Although she did sell Nina and GG's christening necklaces. But you don't miss them, do you, little ones? Good thing me and Dan never got those. And I don't think Tom-tom was ever even christened, yet. But with most stuff, it was always better not to get too much."

"So, what do you get?" I asked.

"Two boxes of cereal," piped up Nina, "and apple juice. Crackers and peanut butter, and two milks."

"Canned soup for dinner," said Dan, making a slight face, "usually chicken and rice or chicken noodle."

"I thought you liked that," said Rodney.

"I do, but it's almost every day," said Dan.

"I like it," said Nina, "because the soup tastes good with the crackers and peanut butter. Don't get tomato."

"We never have much to do with vegetables," Rodney admitted, laughing.

"You never have eggs for breakfast?" I asked.

"Ew, no," said Rodney.

"I like them," Dan said to me in a loud whisper.

I laughed and said, "Me too."

"I would like cookies," said Nina, "but Roddy always says it's too much money."

"Cookies," said GG, suddenly paying close attention, "Yis. Like cookies."

"Wow," said Rodney, "two votes for cookies. Okay, maybe we'll get some. Wilma, do you know what kind of cookie would be good for a little guy like GG?"

"I don't know much about babies, but my mom always used to buy us graham crackers," I said, "Do you guys like them? They taste good, but not too sweet."

"That might be something to try," said Rodney, "and since it's Saturday, and we're out of coffee, we will get that too. And the toilet paper, and diapers. That's our Saturday stuff. And for once, maybe some Hershey's syrup."

"All right," I said, "You're a big spender this week, huh?"

"Well," he said, "something tells me that we might all need a little something special this week."

In the store, we went around the aisles in a group, and the kids got excited over the graham crackers and chocolate syrup. Rodney carefully counted up the money. Six bottles of baby formula, two boxes of cereal, two half gallons of milk, apple juice, cheap peanut butter, saltine crackers and three cans of soup for dinner. How much did it all cost? Plus, a roll of toilet paper. Twenty cents for that, a dollar fifty for milk, fifty cents for cereal, sixty cents for the soup, thirty-eight cents for apple juice, sixty-seven cents for the peanut butter, twenty-two cents for the crackers, plus a dollar thirty-nine for the coffee. The most expensive thing was the baby formula, which was thirty-two cents per bottle, and each boy drank at least three bottles a day, so Rodney bought six at a time for a dollar ninety-two. Also, once a week he bought a large bag of diapers, for three dollars and seventy-five cents each. Rodney brought extra money today, because of the graham crackers, which were seventy-nine cents, and that "expensive" chocolate syrup, which turned out to be only twenty-six cents for a can. Dan and I had to tease him about that. Then I reminded him about the baking soda, so we got two large boxes of that for twenty cents each. The total was twelve dollars and fifty-eight cents.

"You get the money for this from your Mom's welfare check? Is it enough?" I asked.

"We get by. It's not this much every day. Most days it's only about six dollars. I guess we spend about a hundred and eighty dollars on groceries per month, going by a weekly amount of forty-five dollars or so. The food stamps help, so it's important to get Mom into town to get certified for that every month, has to be done by the fifteenth for the following month, and missing that would be a big problem. But with the food stamps, it's a lot easier, and Mom does need some money for her booze, of course. We're lucky to pay only eighty-five dollars for the rent, 'cause Mom knows the landlord and the place is in pretty lousy shape, but it's still a break for us. I get money orders from the post office to pay for the electricity and gas. Usually it's about fifty for that, although in winter the gas goes up, of course, so then it's more like eighty or close to a hundred sometimes. When that happened, I tried to short Mom on her booze money, but that didn't always work, so we had to go without the juice and peanut butter. But we need the gas for the heat, so the babies won't be too cold. And our girl's just got to have her TV shows," he said as he patted Nina's head.

"What about the phone, is that much money?" I asked.

"Not really, but I do consider it an extra expense. We've done without it."

"Wow," I said, wondering how it would feel if I couldn't call Lucy.

"Sometimes it's weird without it," said Rodney, "but if we don't have the phone, I can use the payphone at the store to call Jeff. Just to make sure he knows that I am still going to bug him, even if we don't have phone service."

"He might worry if you didn't. He looked a little worried when you didn't show up at school yesterday," I remembered.

"No kidding," said Rodney, with a smile. "Well, I was talking to him Thursday after school when my mom had that seizure. Maybe he was worried that she had another one, or something."

I figured it might be a good idea to change the subject. "So, you use money orders to pay the bills, and it usually works out okay?"

"Yeah, so far so good. I have to have the heat on for the babies, but I keep it as low as they can deal with, and then I make everyone wear sweatshirts and put blankets on. But forget about turning off the TV. It's okay though, it seems to help everybody get through the day," he said, looking at Nina. "Tell her what your favorite show is, Nina."

She looked up at him with a big smile. "*The Beverly Hillbillies,*" she said.

"We always watch that after I get home from school. Thank God for reruns," he laughed.

The day was getting brighter, on the way to Dan's friend's house, and we began to enjoy the sun on the fields along the road. "Look at those birds, Dan," said Rodney all of a sudden. "A flock of crows. Do they call it a congress of crows, or is that something else?"

"Um," I said, "I think it's a congress of baboons. I remember my Dad said that once."

"Why a congress?" Dan wanted to know.

"That's just what they say when there's a bunch of them," said Terry. "Maybe it is baboons, I can't remember."

I laughed, "I wonder if a congress of baboons would know about the Pentagon Papers."

"I heard something about that at school, but I don't know what it is," said Dan.

"Are you guys Republicans too, like everybody else around here?" I asked.

Rodney laughed a little, and said, "We really don't bother about all that. But I remember you and your McGovern button. You're lucky that people are pretty nice around here."

"Truth is, I probably would've gotten beat up at the school I was at last year, even without the button. The kids were mean at that school. I do feel glad to be here, even though we might be leaving again."

"To tell you the truth, I'm kind of jealous of you, that you might be leaving. Sometimes I wish we could. Do you really like it here that much?" asked Rodney.

"I really do. It's great to have some friends, but mostly it's just so beautiful here. Don't you love looking at Waggoner's Gap from the high school? Isn't that why you guys go up there for lunch?" I asked him, wondering, for the first time, how all that looked to someone who'd lived their whole lives in that place.

"We like to go up there at lunch, if the weather's nice. Like that time you were talking about before, when we walked by you on the stairs on the way up there, and you dropped that big old book of yours," he said, looking at me with the beginning of a snicker on his face.

"Don't you laugh at me," I said, making to hit him, "There's nothing that weird about liking books."

"I like books," said Nina.

"I don't care about them," weighed in Dan.

"Book good," said GG, "like book. How 'bout more?"

"See, there's your evidence. If GG likes books, then books are good. That's all anyone needs to know, right GG?" I said, leaning over to look at him with a big smile.

"The only book he has is *Pat the Bunny*, it's not exactly great literature," smiled Rodney, "but it's true he has looked at it a whole bunch of times, haven't you, G?"

"Book good," repeated GG.

"I bet I could find some more books for him at the church," I said. "They have a kids' library there where you can borrow anything they have for as long as you want."

"I don't know if that's a good idea. They would never get them back, or at least not in one piece. Tom-tom likes books in a different way," said Rodney, smiling again, "in fact, you can't have him around paper of any kind, unless you like confetti."

"And half of it'll wind up in his mouth, won't it, Tom-tom," said Dan to his baby brother.

"They wouldn't care. I'm still going to look. GG would love it," I said. "Anyway, what do you and Jeff talk about up there, besides how weird I am?"

"Besides that, okay, there are other things I guess," he chuckled, avoiding another swipe from me. "I think I said before, we did go camping at Waggoner's Gap once. Way back about four years ago, when Nina was a baby, Daddy Ted used to take me to Boy Scouts, and Jeff was there. We went on one camping trip, and I would really like to do that again someday. Jeff's mother drinks too, like I told you, and he gets fed up sometimes. He wants to get a tent and go out there for a good long time, bring some money and go back to the store for food once a week or so. It would be great."

"Like Tom Sawyer and Huckleberry Finn. Wow, you should at least read *Tom Sawyer*. You would like it," I said.

"They made us read it last year. I couldn't follow all of it. Sometimes he went on for a really long time about stuff that happened at church, or whatever, and it gets boring. I gave up after the dog got bit by the bug. The poor dog," he said, looking sideways at me. I was trying to remember how far into the book that was. Not very far.

"You didn't read any of the part where they wind up on that island, and everybody thinks they drowned?"

"No, the teacher talked about it, but I didn't read it," he said.

"You need to read it again," was all I said. Then I asked, "Does Jeff live around here?"

"No, actually he lives on the other side of Possumtown, closer to the mountains. He gets on a different bus."

"Is that how you got to be friends, in scouts? Did you go to school together back then?"

"Yes, but I remember Jeff even further back. His mom was friends with my mom, at some point, but not anymore. I don't know much about it, neither of them likes to talk about it, but both of them are still in touch with Aunt Donna, I think."

"You call her Aunt Donna too? I thought she was Mandy's aunt," I said, adding, "I met her the other week at Mandy's church. She's nice."

"She has to be, to be friends with both of them," said Rodney, and asked, "Did she say what she does for a living? I really don't know much about her."

"She works for some Catholic house for winos," I said, since that was my best understanding of it. "It sounds like a pretty tough job."

"Maybe being friends with Miranda and Denise prepared her for that," said Rodney.

"Mandy said her mother said that same exact thing," I said.

"Jeff doesn't have brothers or sisters, it's just him and his mom. He told me that he asked her who his father was, and she said he was just some guy she met at a party in Philadelphia. So now he figures he's a smooth, big-city kind of guy. That Wendy Miller better watch out."

"He likes her?"

"Can't you tell? Oh, that's right, you're not in our class. If you were, you would know, he's so obvious about it."

"And you don't like anybody like that?" I had to ask, realizing I was skating on thin ice.

"No," he said slowly, looking at me sideways again. "I kind of like that Susan Dey on the *Partridge Family*, but besides her, I never liked any girl that much until last night." I smiled at him.

"So now what are you going to say to him?" I said, half teasing. Then I said, "Okay, you don't have to tell me. What else do you guys talk about? Did you ever go fishing?"

"Did you?" he asked, laughing, "'Cause it sounded like you were fishing, a minute ago."

"Well, maybe," I said, "but I liked what you said. Seriously, though, if you did go camping like that, you could fish, and then you wouldn't run out of food so fast."

"Maybe if they find out about Mom, we can all go do that and live in a big tent," he said, in a sort of sing-songy tone that gave me the hint that he was joking out of desperation. Truthfully, I don't always get stuff like that. I mean, it actually didn't sound like a bad idea to me.

Then he said, "Meanwhile, back at the ranch, here is Dan's friend's house. Hey Dan," Rodney called out, since Dan was about 30 feet behind us, distracted by a caterpillar that emerged from the grass to cross the sidewalk. "Would you go knock on the door, since they know you and you owe Chris' mom so many nice dinners?"

"And put that caterpillar back in the grass, he's gonna die if the sun gets hot. You want me to do it?" I said, not having to look to know that Rodney was rolling his eyes.

"No, I can do it," said Dan, and laughed, looking at Rodney.

"Two bug lovers, great," muttered Rodney, and he looked at me and I laughed. "No kidding," he continued, "that's good news, so now someone else can help Dan rescue the waterbugs that crawl up the bathtub drain."

"Ha," I said, "you know what, you're right. My mom always wants to kill them, and I used to do that too. But now I catch them in a cup and put them out the window. The poor things. They eat other bugs, you know, so it's actually good to have them around."

"I'd rather deal with the other bugs," said Rodney.

We drew close to Chris' house, a neat, white-painted wooden house with a green roof and shutters. Dan looked at Rodney, who said, "I promise I'll leave as soon as I finish asking about the solid food for GG."

Chapter Thirteen

Many Meetings at Nancy and Al's House

Chris' mom opened the door. "Hi, Dan," she said, "Who's this with you, your brothers and sisters? You guys must be related, you all have the same eyes."

"Hi," said Dan, "this is Rodney, my big brother," he said, patting Rodney's shoulder.

And Rodney put his hand on my shoulder, and said, "This is my girlfriend, Wilma." I beamed at him. Then he reached over and shook her hand. "Nice to meet Chris' mom," he said, "Thanks for feeding Dan and being so nice to him. I hope he's behaving himself over here."

"He's always just great," said Chris' mom, "and Chris loves spending time with Dan, they always have so much fun together. By the way, my name is

Nancy. Who's this beautiful little girl?" She asked, staring at Nina and touching her hair, a bit cautiously. Nina smiled but didn't say anything.

"Nina's four," said Dan, "she can talk but she likes to be quiet. The babies are GG and Tom-tom."

"GG talk," said GG indignantly.

"Well," said Nancy, with a huge smile, "anybody can see that you talk perfectly well. Is it okay if I take you out of the stroller?" She looked at me, then at Rodney.

"Oh," said Rodney, "we don't want to take too much of your time."

"Don't worry about that one bit. Have you had lunch? I didn't think so. I just made a whole bunch of potato salad and we'll put hamburgers and hotdogs on the grill. You can't say no to that."

Dan gave Rodney a look, and Rodney shrugged. "Sounds good to me," he said, with a big smile. Then he added, "Only thing is, we probably ought to take our groceries home first. I don't want the milk to go bad."

"We'll just put that milk in the fridge while you're here. Remind me and I'll get it for you when you leave. It'll be just fine," said Nancy.

I have to admit, it was not easy to say no to Chris' mom. When I asked her later how she met her husband, Al, it turned out to be her favorite subject, and she made a long story of how she and Al had been high-school sweethearts since the days of the sock hops. "We girls wore these puffy skirts and saddle shoes," she said, "and we stood around at the entrance and sideline of the gym, with that crazy old music, like Elvis and Buddy Holly. Mostly we were bored because the boys skulked around, never asking anyone to dance."

"That's just like the dance at the gym that I went to with my friend, Lucy," I said.

"Yeah, I bet it was," Nancy said, "Some things never change. When Al finally asked me, I guess there were only a few other couples dancing. I could smell alcohol on his breath, and I hate alcohol, but he was kind of cute, so I figured why not. But when we started seeing each other, that was the end of his alcohol phase. And if I didn't put my foot down about that, he might be dead by now, because his other big thing was cars, and those two things don't mix, you know? People didn't pay attention to that so much back in those days. But believe me, he would never have survived. Like a lot of boys, he couldn't focus on anything for more than a few seconds. He's still like that, really," she said, whispering the last few sentences.

I was just smiling and nodding, but I was also wondering if she had known Rodney and Jeff's moms, and Aunt Donna. Before I could ask, Nancy continued, "Yeah, he likes to say, 'You may have saved my life, honey, but I guess we'll never know for sure,' but he knows. He doesn't want to admit it because he thinks I would just take total control of everything. But I wouldn't do that. Just once in a while, when he really blows it, I make him sit down and tell me what the hell he thought he was doing. Thank God there's been nothing like that recently."

Later on, when I was talking to Al, and it turned out we were both Tolkien fans, he had his own opinion about his marriage to Nancy. "When I read Tolkien in the late sixties, I thought that me and Nancy were a lot like Arwen and Aragorn," he said, "except Tolkien left out writing about their married life, where Arwen would have sat Aragorn down and told him what was gonna be what. 'No more pipes with funny tobacco for you,' she would have said, and you know what? He would have put up and shut up, like any other guy with a wife."

I told him he was probably right about them, and we agreed that there wasn't enough information about the women in those books. But when I told him my idea of adding a human female character, his eyes started to glaze over, so I decided to drop the subject. Then I suddenly remembered Lucy and her mom, Mary. "Can I make a phone call?" I asked him, "I can't believe I forgot that my friend and her mom were coming to Rodney's house to bring us fried chicken. I hope I can catch them before they leave home."

"Why don't you invite them over here?" said Al. "It would be nice to meet your friends, and we like fried chicken too."

"That would be great, if you're sure it's all right," I said, "thank you for inviting them."

"No problem," said Al, "and while you're calling them, I'm going to see if some of those hot dogs and burgers are done. We've got hungry kids to feed," he added, grinning.

The smell of the grilling food was reminding me that I didn't eat breakfast, and I was glad to hear the sound of dishes and food landing on the table in the next room. Al and Nancy's kids came to help serve (and eat) the food, a boy about ten years old like

Dan, presumably his friend Chris, and Chris' sister, named Molly, who looked to be about seven years old. Molly had brown hair like Al, while Chris was blond, like his mother.

I called Lucy and her mom, and I was lucky to find that they were just leaving their house. Since it wasn't that far from Al and Nancy's house, they were with us before long. They were both pretty amazed that I was there with Rodney and his little siblings. Lucy drew me aside as soon as she could and asked, "So, when did you go over there? This morning, or when?"

She was being casual about it, but I could tell she was concerned, and although Mary was talking to Nancy, I could almost feel her ears straining to hear what we were saying. Occasionally she turned to give me a glare that was almost, but not quite, cross-eyed. I was scared to say anything, so I just pulled Lucy back into the living room to watch the babies with me. Both babies were making their way around the living room and Nancy turned to watch them with us, entranced. GG was a huge hit, picking up a snow globe and saying "Snow? That not snow," with a sober judge-like scowl.

Tom-tom just made with the babbling, which always seemed to get ladies' attention, as Rodney pointed out. "One thing you have to admit, my Mom made cute babies," he said to me, and I had to agree.

While Al was serving the burgers and Mary brought her fried chicken to the table, Nancy came over to Rodney and asked, "What are these wonderful baby boys eating these days? Can I put some of the chicken in the blender for them?"

"You know, I wanted to ask you about that. I've been giving them formula, but someone said they should be eating regular food, and GG is interested."

Nancy gasped. "GG hasn't been eating solid food? He should have been doing that for almost a year now."

"Oh my God," exclaimed Mary, and then added to Nancy, "You know, if they don't start eating solids by the time they're about a year old or so, they might never take to it. I have a cousin who kept giving her baby cereal from a bottle till he was almost three, and that boy wouldn't eat anything more solid than mashed potatoes until he was almost a teenager. He still won't eat steak, or a hamburger, or even chicken."

Al looked at her with real alarm. "Wow," he said, "life without hamburgers."

"I know," said Mary, and they both started laughing.

Rodney looked up at Nancy, embarrassed. "I gave GG some cereal this morning, and he liked it. I would have started sooner, but I wasn't sure what to do. Dan was the one who said I should ask you about it."

"Well, that was smart of him," said Nancy, smiling, "he is such a thoughtful boy sometimes, I've noticed that. Don't worry, we will talk about it. For today, how about if I put some of this food in the blender for them? They might enjoy it for a change."

"That would be nice," said Rodney, smiling, and added, "those hot dogs smell amazing."

"Well you relax and serve yourself. I will take care of the babies, just give me a minute to blend the food."

By this time, we were all taking seats and reaching for hot dogs, which was the first thing to be served up. Then we passed Mary's potato salad and chicken around, and the air was filled with the sound of contented munching and gulping.

Nancy returned with the food for the babies. She sat down next to Rodney and put GG on her other side, with Tom-tom in her lap. Then she asked Rodney, "So how is your Mom doing?"

He had two hot dogs with mustard on his plate already and was half way through the first one, so he took a minute to speak. Next to him on the other side, Dan had already finished a hot dog, eating it in three bites, like a wolf cub.

"She's okay," said Rodney, nodding, still with food in his mouth. "She just needs a rest. She had a bad night."

He looked like he was sorry he said that, as Nancy's eyes narrowed and she said "You know, I went to school with Miranda, I do remember some things about her. Still drinks a bit, does she?"

Quickly changing the subject, Rodney said, "You know who else said they knew her in high school, was our new neighbor, John Smith."

"John Smith," said Nancy, "A big guy with dark hair? You're kidding me. I can't believe he's still alive. Wasn't he in jail or something? Honey," she yelled to Al, who was watching the grill.

"What's up?" he called out, and smiled, but then winced, rubbing his forehead.

"What do you remember about John Smith?"

Al frowned. "Not much. Nothing good. Who needs to know?"

"He's living near Miranda's house," said Nancy.

Al looked serious all of a sudden. "Really? Since when?"

"Not more than a week," said Rodney.

"He's right next door to them," I added, between mouthfuls of Mary's peerless potato salad.

Nancy gasped a little. Mary, who had been listening to all this with her eyes wide and her mouth just slightly open, now said, "We went over there Thursday, and he shook my hand. Nancy, I am not kidding you, I got chills when he touched me. He is scary. I can't believe this nice young man, with all these little ones with him, has to deal with living right next door to that scary man."

"Wow, Mary," Nancy said, "if he touched me, I would probably scream. You are so brave."

"Also, this fried chicken is the best I've ever tasted," said Rodney, changing the subject again, "and the potato salad too. Wilma was right when she said how good your cooking is, Mary. Thank you so much."

Mary beamed. "Are all of you kids getting enough? What about your little sister, Rodney?" she asked, looking at Nina.

Nina looked up at her, waving a drumstick, her eyes glowing. "So good," she said, with a grateful smile, and Mary smiled back and put two more drumsticks on her plate.

Nancy had been spooning food into Tom-tom's mouth while she was talking, and looking to make sure GG didn't drop his spoon. They had big mounds of blended chicken, with blended potato salad and apple sauce on the side, to round out their feast. When Nancy had to get up for a second, I took over with Tom-tom, putting him in my lap. Rodney was watching this with a bemused smile, saying, "Wow, they've never eaten like this before. I sure hope they don't throw up."

Nancy laughed and said, "Don't even say that, Rodney," and Mary looked over and laughed too, saying, "Well it's something new for them, but they're old enough, they should be okay. Try GG with some pieces of banana or cheese, see how he does with the chewing."

Meanwhile, Al looked thoughtful. "Well," he said, "John Smith might have only just got out of jail," said Al, "How long was he in jail for, Nance?"

Nancy looked blank, and said, "Al, I barely paid attention to any of that."

Her husband said, "I paid some attention. I think it was maybe ten years, or a bit less."

Rodney gasped. "He said his wife was coming today, bringing little kids," he said.

Al stared at him for a second, then said, "Well, they might not be John's kids."

"Was he really in jail for murder?" Rodney wanted to know.

"Yes," said Al, "Wasn't that on the radio? He killed some guy."

"I heard it," I said, "and I read this thing in an old paper that he might have killed his parents, too. That wasn't for sure, but it looked suspicious."

Mary stared at me. "That's right, honey, Lucy told me you went over to the College Library and looked that up. You're smart. So, what did you do, run over to this nice boy's house to tell him about it? When did you do that? I was just wondering," she said, her tone dead serious.

I looked at Rodney in a panic. He looked nonchalant, saying, "She was with us this morning, and it was a big help, since we needed to make a big shopping trip. We would have had a lot more trouble without her. She called home, her family knows about it."

I just looked at the ground. It was amazing to me that he could think of the right thing to say at a time like this. He continued to look unruffled, and finessing another change of subject, he said, "My Mom recognized John Smith when he moved in next door, she remembered him from high school, too. She told me he was mean, but he seems pretty nice when he's talking to us sometimes. How does a guy like that become a murderer?"

Al looked down. "Only God knows, but I don't think he was happy when he was really young. Nancy won't remember, but I knew him in elementary school. He used to look so sad and quiet, and in kindergarten he even started crying over nothing sometimes. Then as he got bigger, he got meaner and started picking on people. Later on, when we were all in gym together at the high school, other kids said they saw scars from a whip on his back."

"Oh, man," exclaimed Rodney, "there's a kid at school with us right now like that."

"Oh, the poor kid, that's awful. Can't the school do something?" Mary wanted to know.

"I don't know," said Rodney. "Anyway, that kid isn't mean. Just kind of quiet."

"Poor kid," said Nancy, "I wonder if there's any point in contacting the welfare people about that. He ought to be removed from his home."

"Except you don't know what the foster home would be like," added Al. "Kids sometimes get brutalized in those places even more so."

Rodney looked at me, his eyes wide with concern, and I looked back, remembering what he said about how anything was better than having the little ones wind up in foster care. Even that kid in school. I knew who he was talking about, even us girls knew about that. Awful as it was for anyone to be whipped, who knows whether he would be worse off in some stranger's home. Finally, I said, "I feel so bad for that kid, and it feels weird to think that John Smith was in the same boat. I almost feel sorry for him."

Rodney said, "I don't think I could really feel sorry for John Smith. Maybe I would have, if he hadn't been mean to my Mom and her friends, in high school. I know my mom really didn't like the guy, and she almost never has anything bad to say about anybody."

"I have to admit, he was kind of a jerk and not many people liked him," said Al, "but I can't forget, when I think about him, how he must have got beaten when he was little. I don't know if that is the reason that he acted like he did."

"And his parents wound up dead, too," I reminded them. "That seems even more suspicious, knowing that they treated him like that."

"Maybe there's even some kind of justice to that," said Al. "Anyway, I'm surprised John Smith's wife is back, especially with two kids in tow. Would she be safe, do you suppose? Did you ever talk with her, Nance?"

He looked at his wife who shrugged. "Not really. I met her once, maybe at one of the reunions. She was younger than us, I remember that much. Kind of chunky, blonde, not too smart."

"That's about half the women in central PA," chortled Al.

Nancy hit Al's butt lightly with a newspaper, and said, "You better not mean me. Anyway, I lost 20 pounds on the grapefruit diet, don't forget that."

Al shrugged, but Mary' eyes were bulging again. "Really," she said, "I have got to try that. Twenty pounds, that's at least one dress size, right?"

"More like two," said Nancy, "I went from a twelve to an eight."

"Some of those eights are kind of tight though," ventured Al, who winced when Nancy glared at him.

"Well, one dress size would get me down to a twelve," said Mary, "and I would love to be a twelve again. I am going to try that."

"Don't get the grapefruit at the store in Possumtown, though. You have to go into town," said Nancy. "Okay, let me think. There was one reunion where we saw pretty much everybody who graduated with us, and that was 1965, the fifth one. Only eight years ago, wow, it seems like such a long time. Most of us had kids already. Miranda was there with her husband, that football player that drank a lot, and that guy John Smith brought his wife. I remember she was wearing a pink sheath dress that looked nice with her long blond hair. I had mine in a flipped hair-style and I was wearing a blue flowered cotton frock with matching blue pumps. Not very fancy, but it was the best outfit I had at the time and I loved it, to tell you the truth."

"It sounds adorable," said Mary. "I have a blue dress kind of like that, but I don't think it fits anymore. That sounds like fun. What were the other girls wearing?"

"Well, if I remember right, Denise wore a little black dress, like Audrey Hepburn in *Breakfast at Tiffany's*, you know? Only shorter, sort of below-the-knee length. And it really looked good on her. Miranda was wearing an ivory sheath that looked like it might have been her wedding dress, but she looked great, too. Denise made a total fool of herself as soon as she saw John, even though she brought Donna with her. Finally, she left with some paunchy guy from the 20th reunion party in the next ballroom over, and Donna had to ask us for a ride back to her parents' house. Do you remember that, Al?"

"Well, I remember driving her home, and I also remember that there was kind of a sad situation that happened with Miranda's husband and John. I think John was following Miranda around, even with his wife in tow, and Miranda was refusing to acknowledge his existence. After a while, John went to talk to her husband, buying him drink after drink. Maybe he was getting him drunk to get back at Miranda. When she wanted to leave, her husband was out in the front of the hotel with John Smith, and the two men were play-wrestling in the fountain at the entrance. John had got the guy in a half nelson and was holding his head under the stream of water, so he was gasping for air, and Miranda got really upset. She ran up screaming and took a swing at John's face with her pocketbook, yelling, 'Stop that, you horrible man!' or something like that. She was screaming so hard she made herself fall over in the water and I think she might have gone under it for a second. So, John just walked away, and her husband said, 'But Miranda, we were just joking around. He said he was going to help me sober up.'"

"How did you happen to see all that?" asked Nancy. "I don't remember any of it."

"I was out front of the hotel, waiting for you," said Al.

"Waiting for me, huh? You weren't smoking something?" said Nancy.

"Well, I don't remember that, it was a long time ago. Anyway, I couldn't help wondering why Miranda got all upset like that. She was really exploding, I was so surprised. You know, Rodney, I hope you didn't mind hearing all that. I keep forgetting that this is your mother we're talking about."

"It's okay," said Rodney, with one of his half-smiles. "I think I know why she got like that. She has a kind of a problem with water. Especially if she got her head under water. That would really make her upset."

"Come to think of it, the murder happened that year," said Al, "sometime in the fall, I think. Or maybe late summer. Some bait store, down by Boiling Springs, where Smith was working. I don't remember who he killed, though. Seems like it was someone else from our school, but I can't remember who."

Mary looked at Lucy, and Lucy looked at me. I shook my head just a little. I did not remember if Rodney said that he knew that Smith had murdered his dad, and I didn't want it to come out this way. Then I thought it over. Did we ever talk about it? It seemed like he would know something like that. For sure, his mother would have known. Even so, better not to bring it up now.

Meanwhile Rodney asked Al, "Do you remember some blond guy named Jerry? Did he go to school with you too? Has a ponytail now?"

Al stared at him. "I have seen a guy who looks like that over by the store, with a long blond ponytail. He looks high most of the time. Why do you ask?"

Dan blurted out, "He tried to be with my Mom, but she didn't like him."

Rodney said, "Okay, Dan. We did have kind of a long night. I was just curious if you knew that guy, that's all. He was kind of hanging around for the last week or so, but, well, never mind."

Al looked thoughtful. "Maybe we've talked about these characters enough. Do you think it might be time for some ice cream?"

Nina's eyes went huge, and Dan smiled bigger than I thought he would have been able to, even with that big mouth of his. Rodney looked around at his sister and brothers and beamed, "Wow, thanks, Al. That will be another new experience for the babies."

"I can't wait to see their faces when they try it," said Nancy.

Bowls and spoons were passed, and at least five cartons of various flavors came out of the freezer. Nina and the little ones were exclaiming with joy, while Rodney dished out ice cream for them and a double helping for Dan, who immediately started shoveling it in. Rodney turned to Nancy and said, "This is so nice. I can't thank you enough."

She smiled and clapped him on the shoulder, saying, "It's our pleasure. It makes me so happy just watching you guys eat, and it's wonderful to have babies to feed again. I didn't realize how much I missed that."

Then she suddenly frowned, and said, "I still don't understand why they were only getting formula all this time. Didn't your mom do anything about that? Boy, I'd really like to talk with that Miranda. How about if I drive you home and I can talk to her for a minute?"

"No, no need, we will be fine walking," said Rodney, paling visibly. "She's very tired."

"I'll just bet she is," said Nancy with a frown. "I'm coming over there to talk to her sometime soon, you bet. Alright, not today, if you don't want me to. But take some cookies, when you leave, and chips. Along with that milk, of course. I will get it out of the fridge. Anything else you might need? You kids haven't been eating enough."

"Cookies," cried Nina, her eyes springing wide. "Oh, thank you," she said, and got up to hug Nancy impulsively.

Rodney stared at her, looking amazed. "So adorable, right?" I said to him, with a smile, and he said, "I've never seen her just go and hug somebody like that before."

Rodney got up too, and I followed, holding Tom-tom. GG was still spooning the last of his icecream, but Rodney went to get the stroller for Tom-tom, preparing his family to go back home.

"So, you kids are leaving?" asked Mary, "I'm so glad we got to know you better. I would give you all a ride, but the car's kind of small and I don't think both strollers would fit. We have clothes for the little ones, but not for you and your brother yet, so we didn't bring them today, but sometime during the week we want to come by and bring clothes for all of you."

"That's so nice of you, but you don't need to do that," said Rodney.

"It's our pleasure, and we will really enjoy doing that, so please let us come. Probably Wednesday, but Thursday at the latest. Okay?"

"Well, that's very kind, but…" he looked at Nina, who was smiling at him like it was Christmas, and added, "well, okay, that sounds very nice," but he looked uncomfortable.

To me, she said, "We can give you a ride home, Wilma," in a tone that indicated that I was meant to say yes to that. So, without thinking it through much, I agreed, and gave Nina and the babies each a big hug goodbye. I almost hugged Rodney too, but we both got self-conscious with everybody watching, so I just patted him on the shoulder and said, "Hey, be careful, all right?" and he just looked at me, and said he would.

We helped him put the babies in the strollers and pack up his groceries, as well as the cookies and chips and bananas and a few other things Nancy made him take. The bags looked really full, but we were pretty sure he would get them home all right. Dan was playing somewhere with his friend, so Rodney got Nina to push her own stroller while he pushed the babies. Nancy almost insisted on driving them when she saw that, and then she offered to go find Dan, but Rodney said not to do that, that they did this often and it wasn't that far. Nina smiled and seemed happy to push the stroller, but I walked with them for part of the way to the corner and pushed it with her.

"I guess I'll see you Monday at school," I said to Rodney. "Can you call me tomorrow and let me know how you're doing? I hope that man doesn't bother you. Seriously, let me know if you need help."

Rodney laughed and said, "In fact, I probably couldn't stop you from helping, whether we needed it or not." He smiled at me and added, "We'll be alright. I guess I have to make a decision about Mom at some point. Tell you what, I'll call you and let you know what I decide, see what you think about it. Does that sound okay?"

"Yeah," I said, "that would be great," and looked at him, thinking how it didn't feel like I should be leaving, but not knowing how to get out of it. He reached over and kissed me lightly on the lips, then sort of patted my shoulder and left.

Chapter Fourteen

Nina Makes a Joke

I turned and walked back, turning around a couple of times to wave to Nina, who was looking back, and it wasn't till I was almost back to Mary's car that I remembered the bike. With a strange sense of relief, I looked in the car and saw clearly that they didn't have room to put the bike in there.

"You guys, I'm so sorry I forgot, but I rode my bike over here and left it at Rodney's house. I have to go back for it. You can't put it in your car, so I guess I have to ride it home. It's no problem, but I can't just leave it there."

"Why not?" said Mary, "Can't you just come back later with one of your parents and pick it up? Why do you have to ride it all the way home again?"

"The thing is, it's not exactly at Rodney's house. I left it in the woods across the street from his house, he doesn't even know where it is. If anybody sees it, they could just take it."

"Why'd you do that?" asked Lucy, sounding a bit like her mother.

"It's a long story. Believe me it's no trouble, I'll just ride it home like I rode it over there, I know the way, it won't be hard."

"Well, you better not hang around over there. We'll be expecting a phone call from you this afternoon, you understand?" said Mary, with her eyes beginning to bulge again.

"Don't worry, I will," I said, not really sure but willing to say anything to get out of the line of fire. "I better go get it before somebody steals it."

Saying this, I started walking down the road the way Rodney went. He and Nina had already turned right down their road, but I could see Dan was ahead of me, with some surprise, since I didn't notice him leave. He must have walked past while I was talking with Mary and Lucy. He was going fast, too, almost running, and I couldn't catch up. So, it was a bit like a parade, with Rodney, Nina and the babies leading the way, Dan following them, and me in the rear. After I turned the corner, I could see Rodney's house, and I could also see John Smith walking away from Rodney's house toward his own. I figured that Rodney and the kids were in their house already. I had already made up my mind to stop and see how they were before I went home, so I figured, now I had a good reason. I wanted to know what that man was saying to Rodney. I didn't even look for the bike.

I went up to the house, and the door was a little bit open, so I went up to it and called out to them, "Hey you guys, are you okay? I had to come back to get my bike."

"You better come in, quick," said Rodney, "it's better if he doesn't see you."

I walked in, and Dan, who looked like he'd been crying, ran up and gave me a big hug. "I'm glad you came back," he said, "I couldn't believe you'd just go home and leave us."

I hugged him back and laughed, "Well, I guess I will have to go home some time. But I'm glad I came back too. It's going to be okay, Dan. We just have to figure out what to do next."

"That's right," said Rodney, "and I'm glad you came back too, because we really need your help. I want you to take Dan and Nina and the babies back to Chris' house."

"And you're going to stay here?" I asked him. "That doesn't sound like a good idea. You won't be safe here by yourself."

"I won't be alone. Mom's here, remember?" said Rodney, and Dan gave him a funny look.

"Oh," I said, "I get it." I guessed that he didn't want John Smith to discover his Mom's body while we were gone. "Okay, I'll take them. What happened, anyway?"

"Well, we just got back when we heard his wife screaming next door, something like, don't you talk to my kids that way, and then we heard a slamming door and the sound of a little kid wailing. Then John came outside and saw me staring at his house, so he started coming over here. I got Nina and the babies in the house, set them down in front of the TV with bottles and cookies before I heard him knocking on the door. He really made me jump, he knocked so loud. Then he said that he tried to speak to Mom while we were gone, but no matter how loud he knocked or yelled, she didn't come, and he didn't hear her say anything. He was like, are you sure she's all right, and I said yes, and he said okay, but he was beginning to think that I wasn't telling him something, and then he waved through the screen door at the babies, to freak me out, I guess. Dan got upset when he was coming back and saw that John was here, and so he ran and hid behind the house until John left."

Dan looked embarrassed at this, so I said, "I don't blame you, he scares me too."

Then Rodney went on, "We heard another scream just a few minutes ago, right before you got here. You didn't go over there and scare them, did you?"

"Very funny," I said, but I didn't like the idea of him staying in that house next door to that man. "Please come with us."

"I just think I need to stay here and watch Mom. I'll clear out if things get scary," he added.

"Okay. As long as you're really going to do that. Do we need to pack up and get ready?"

Dan said, "Let's get Nina's Barbies and my comic books, too."

"Right, go get them," said Rodney.

They got the strollers and we made sure both boys had clean diapers.

"Wait," said GG, "get cereal. Get Tom-Tom blankie."

"Okay," said Dan, "I'm putting them right here behind you. How about *Pat the Bunny*?"

"Yis."

"Okay, *Pat the Bunny* too. You want your truck?" asked Dan.

"No. Go soon." GG looked concerned.

"You are so right, GG. We do need to go soon," said Rodney. "Nina, you got your dolls? Ready?"

She nodded, went to hug him and started to cry. Rodney got a towel from the kitchen and handed it to her, then knelt down and hugged her again. I almost started to cry, too.

"I'll be all right," said Rodney. "you just listen to Wilma and Dan, okay? I'll be with you soon, but I have to stay right here now and help Mom."

The walk to Chris' house took about twenty minutes, less if you didn't have a stroller to push, but it seemed a lot longer that day. To cheer Nina up, I asked her more questions about her Barbie dolls, and then I asked Dan what he did when he was at Chris' house. He made it sound so good, she was listening with her eyes wide and it looked like GG was listening too. They got excited when he said that Chris' mom actually baked cookies herself sometimes.

"She makes them herself, right, not that store-bought cookie dough," I said. "So, I think you guys are going to have such a good time, I mean, we had so much fun at lunch," in the brightest tone I could muster up. I knocked on the door.

"Oh hi," said Nancy, sounding surprised. "You guys are back. We were just cleaning up from lunch. What happened?"

"Oh, well," I said awkwardly, "We just had so much fun at lunch, we had to come back and tell you how great it was. Hope you don't mind."

"No, of course not," said Nancy, "I'm always so happy to see all of you, especially Tom-tom and GG," she said, giving them a big smile.

"Well yes, they are so popular," I said, "and in big demand everywhere, but they honestly don't care about all those other people, they just love you."

"And cookies," said GG.

"I love how honest you are, GG," said Nancy, laughing.

"I love cookies too," said Nina with an extra cute smile, "oh, and you of course."

"Wow, Nina, are you making a joke? So funny," I smiled at her, and then said to Nancy, "Rodney would be amazed that Nina told a joke. Good for you, Nina."

"So, come in already," said Nancy, pushing the strollers in and taking the babies out of them. She took them into the kitchen and gave them a cookie each, and while they were snacking Dan went and found Chris, and I told Nancy what had happened. "So, I hope you don't mind if I leave the kids with you for a while. I have to go back to see how Rodney is doing. I can't leave him there to deal with that guy by himself. Anyway, my bike is still there"

"I can't help feeling like you'd be better off staying here, Wilma. What can you do about a big man like John Smith?" she wanted to know.

"Well, yeah, but what can Rodney do either? I don't think anything's going to happen. I'm just going back to check, and then I'll ride my bike home like I was supposed to. I'd be surprised if Mary hasn't called my parents by now. I'd better go. I'm sure Rodney will come back for the kids when he thinks it's safe."

"They're welcome here as long as they need to stay," said Nancy.

"Maybe I'll just leave quickly," I said. "I don't want to make them upset."

"Oh, I think you better say good bye to the little ones," said Nancy. "They are smart kids, they'll notice it if you don't."

"I guess you're right," I said, smiling sheepishly, and went into the kitchen. "Okay, you guys, I have to go check on Rodney. You know I can't leave him there by himself, and anyway I have to get my bike and go home. But I'm going to call you soon. And sometime this week me and Mary and Lucy are coming over with clothes for you guys."

I gave each of them a little hug and kiss, and said bye one more time, close to tears. Nina looked up and said, "It's okay, Wilma. We're gonna see you. Love," and blew a kiss.

Then the tears did come, and I blew a kiss back. I headed out the door, wiping my eyes with the back of my hand, and Nancy said, "Be careful, Wilma."

I called out, "I will," as I went off running down the street.

I turned the corner and kept running until I saw the blue truck pull out of the neighbor's driveway. I jumped into the side of the road and hid behind a tree, noticing with some surprise that this was where I'd left my bicycle. After the truck went by, I went up to the house, knocked, opened the door and called, "Hey, Rodney, what's going on now?"

Chapter Fifteen

Baking Soda

I almost gasped as he emerged from the room at the end of the hall where his mother lay.

"Oh, wow, you've been in there. Are you all right?" I asked.

"It's okay if you have no sense of smell. What were we going to use the baking soda for again?"

"I thought we could put it on her body kind of like talcum powder and it might help with the smell. You want to try it? Where's the baking soda?"

"In the kitchen."

I went in, found it on the counter, and brought both boxes to him.

"Here," I said, "you take one and I'll take one and we'll both put it on her on either side."

"I have to warn you," he said, "she's not looking her best."

He lifted the towel from her face and my whole body jerked back as I gasped. Her face had transformed, the sagging flesh draped over the once chiseled cheekbones like fleshy gelatin. She looked like an alien dressed as a Barbie doll. And she certainly was beginning to smell.

"Wow, Mom," said Rodney, sounding a little more cheerful, "We have to do something about you."

He took the box of baking soda and started pouring it on her hair, under her shirt, anywhere it wouldn't show too much, using an entire large box, and I did the same on the other side. "A girl can never have too much baking soda, especially when she smells like this. Sorry if it makes you look pale," Rodney said. "Okay, what else can we do to spruce her up? Too late for eyeshadow."

I had to giggle a little. "Yeah, the way her eyelids look, I don't think we have enough."

He looked at me, balefully, like I just picked my nose or something, and then he started giggling too. "Well," he said, "what can we do to make her look prettier? How about her scarf?"

He went to the box in the living room where they stored his mother's clothes and a few other belongings including a brush, her make-up bag, an old pink bottle of perfume called Ambush that was almost empty, her scarf, which was a filmy turquoise blue, and the matching round blue sunglasses. He put these on her, and she almost looked alive. I said, "It does make me feel better to see her looking a little nicer," and he agreed.

"You know", he said, "John was here right before you got back."

"I saw his truck go down the road. Did he say where he was going?"

"No, he didn't, but his wife is still in the house with her kids. They had a huge fight before he left. Then he came over here, smelling drunk, and wanted to talk to Mom again.

I told him that she didn't want to see anyone, that she keeps complaining she doesn't look like herself. He said to tell her he said hello, and that he remembered how beautiful she was in high school."

"Great," I said, "not enough that he's creepy and dangerous, now he's trying to flirt."

"Then I asked him if everything was okay with his wife," said Rodney, "and he said something like how women take time to get accustomed to things, and that she never was a good listener. Then he asked me if I needed a hand with the plumbing. I guess he smelled Mom. Then he left, thank God. I was dying to get him out of here, if you know what I mean."

He looked at me and we both laughed, a kind of weird laugh that was almost crying. I gave him a hug. We sat down on the couch and Rodney said, "I've been trying to figure the guy out. It seems like, no matter how strange he seems to us, he feels like he has a right to act the way he does, and I don't understand why. Why do some men abuse and make fun of women? I know I don't ever want to be like that."

"I was wondering about that too," I said, "and I was wondering if some men act like that because they're afraid of how women can make them feel. A guy like him wouldn't like being made to feel bad, especially since his parents were mean to him."

"Maybe it's kind of like the way some men feel okay about hurting animals, or hunting them for food, even if they don't need food at all. Of course, around here lots of people do that, women too."

I was silent on that one, thinking of our two heifers. Then I said, "Maybe he decided not to care about people, because not caring gives you a kind of an edge.

Like, it's probably easier to get people to do what you want if you don't care that much. I've noticed that about my Dad, when he's selling insurance."

"But the thing about John Smith, he does care about my mother. Probably ever since high school."

"Sad for him," I said, "no matter how much you like somebody, you can't make them like you."

I looked at Rodney, thoughtfully. He was looking at his mother. "Yeah," he finally said, "too bad for John Smith. I guess the one person he really cared about just didn't like him, and there was nothing he could do about it. Well, let's get a drink of water and think about what to do next."

He went and got two glasses of water, gave me one, took another big breath and took a sip of water, and began to look like he felt a little better. "Okay", he said, "how can we help his wife? We can't just leave her to deal with him alone when he gets back. He might beat her or something worse, even. I can't listen to that." He looked at me frantically.

"Okay," I said, "good idea. We better hurry up. We'll figure out what to do when we get there." So we jumped up and ran through some bushes and weeds straight to the neighbors' house and knocked frantically.

Chapter Sixteen

Julie from Harrisburg

The house was wood, with faded white paint that needed touching up, like Rodney's house. But this was a two-story house, although the upstairs windows, with crumbling sashes and cobwebs over the ancient half-screens, looked unopened and unused. The screen on the screen door had been broken and taped back, on the left side.

"Hello," said John Smith's wife, as she opened the door a crack, and seeing Rodney and me, she opened it more whispering, "Come in. You live next door, right? I saw you when we got here," she continued, looking at Rodney.

She was wearing a bath robe over a nightgown with a yard of thick blonde hair, her round blue eyes in her round face full of fear. "I am just trying to get my kids together to get out of here," she said and showed us two toddlers, a boy with hair and eyes like hers, who might be three, and a tiny girl of about one with a mess of dark hair and shiny dark eyes.

"We'll help you," said Rodney, "I'm Rodney, and this is Wilma. Do you have a place to go?"

"No. My family is all the way in Harrisburg. I would need a car, and I don't have one. I thought of going to the police station, but I don't even know where it is. I wish I'd never come here, but John can be so charming when he wants to be, you know?"

Rodney looked like he couldn't imagine when that would be, and I couldn't either, honestly. "We'll get your boy ready while you put the baby in the stroller," he said. "I have an idea of where you can go. Do you know how much time we have?"

She stood still, transfixed with the effort of thinking, then looked up. "Maybe forty-five minutes. It takes him about an hour to get there and back, if I'm right about where he went."

"We have to move fast. This house is a twenty-minute walk and I don't want him to see you walking. Let's go. By the way, how far is Harrisburg?"

"About thirty miles. I never should have come here without a car. This was never a great idea, but with a car at least I could just leave whenever I wanted to. Not now. I guess he liked that idea."

"Have you talked to your family recently?" I asked, "do they know you might be coming?"

"No, I didn't get the chance. I don't have time to call them right now, do I?"

"No, not at all," said Rodney firmly. "We really need to hurry."

In a few minutes we had the kids ready and were heading out the door. "We'll walk you up to the main road, then I'll point out the house to you," said Rodney, "It's to the left. You can see it from the corner."

"Great. Thank you so much, I can't tell you how much this means, not just for me but for my kids," she said, stifling a sob.

"So," asked Rodney as we began walking, "these are not John's kids? But you and John were married before he went to jail?"

"Only for a little while. He is older than me. I was only eighteen and he was twenty-three. He was in Vietnam, you know."

"Yeah, so was my Dad," said Rodney.

"My dad was in WW II," I said, but they both ignored me.

Julie continued, "Part of the reason he didn't like my brother is because my brother didn't go to Vietnam. He got excused for psychiatric reasons. He might have been accepted later on when they lowered the bar a little, but by that time he didn't want to go and kept moving here and there to avoid getting drafted. He was talking about Canada, but we're glad he didn't have to go there. I'm so glad they ended the draft in January, aren't you?"

"God, yes," said Rodney.

"How old are you?" asked Julie.

"Thirteen," said Rodney.

"You're so mature, I thought you were older than that. My boy is like that, everybody thinks he's older than he is, except that's because he's big for his age, not because of the way he acts, like you. I think he's going to be tall. His dad is tall, but not as tall as John. What do you think? He's only two-and-a-half."

"He's tall alright. This bag is a little heavy. No, it's fine," Rodney said, as she offered to take it.

"That's our miscellaneous bag," she said, "with the kids' toys and my make-up bag and hair stuff, and my Bible."

"Do you read the Bible?" I asked.

"I like to read the New Testament part, about Jesus. It calms me down. We never went to church regularly, but my best friend in school was a Mennonite, and she gave me a Bible and got me reading it."

"I started reading it when we were going to church in Philadelphia. I really liked that church. I guess it's about the only thing I liked about living there," I said.

"Do you have any Mennonites at your school?" asked Julie.

"We have three," I said. "They're nice girls, and I'm friends with one of them. I don't think she likes wearing those little lace caps much."

"No, my friend didn't either. Especially when it was hot out." Then she added, "So Rodney, is Wilma your girlfriend?"

Rodney looked at me and blushed. "Well, I guess she is, as of yesterday."

I smiled and said, "It's kind of a new thing for us."

"Wow," she said. "I'm so happy for you guys."

She poked Rodney a little with her bag and said, "I hope you're a gentleman, not getting too carried away or anything." She giggled, while Rodney rolled his eyes, and I had to giggle, too.

"Don't worry, he's nice," I said with a smile.

"Good," she said, "stick with him, cause a lot of them aren't."

"Listen," said Rodney, "we really have to hurry. Anyway, where does your brother live now?"

"Well, I think he might be around here, at least sometimes. This is where he was, the last time he called us. The thing is, he kind of broke everybody's heart, because he used to do drugs and drink, and then he stopped, and he was doing so well. If he was still sober, I probably would still be in Harrisburg. To be honest, I was hoping I could find him and try to help him, when I got here. But I can't stay in this house with this man." She stopped and blew her nose.

"Are you okay?" asked Rodney.

"Yes. It's just hard because we were so proud of my brother, because he got sober. I think he meant to hang around and help me with the kids. We would have had so much fun together, you know. He is such a nice man, really. Great with kids. I hope he can get sober again and have a few of his own. But it won't be easy, because once he's drinking, that's it, it could take a really long time for him to come back to himself. He's so moody, you couldn't believe how his moods could change."

Suddenly Rodney asked her, "Did you tell me his name?"

"His name's Jerry. He has long hair like mine, wears it in a ponytail all the time. You'd know him if you saw him."

Rodney almost dropped the bag he was carrying and looked at me. I stared back. He shook his head slightly, and I nodded. Then he looked at Julie again. We were almost at the top of the road. There wasn't much time left.

"You really have to get a move on, Julie. Get these kids safe. It's the white and green house. Down there. About a ten-minute walk. Wilma, will you go with her and take the bag?"

"Actually," I said, "I think she'll be okay. Julie, can you take the bag that far?"

"Sure," said Julie, "you kids go do whatever you need to do. But just stay away from John, okay? Seriously. He's dangerous. Doesn't always look that way, but he is."

"Yeah, Wilma, I just think you should go with them and let me do this myself," said Rodney, "I'm trying to think of something to keep him around the house, so he doesn't go after Julie right away. But Julie, you have to tell Chris' parents that you need to get out of here and back to Harrisburg tonight, as soon as you can. The farther away and the faster, the better."

"Harrisburg tonight, that would be great," she looked at him, and tears came to her eyes. Then she said, "Be careful. Don't you think you should both come along with us? He's a big man, and you're just a skinny kid. He could tear you to pieces. I don't like this at all."

Rodney just shook his head, then patted her on the shoulder and pointed her to Chris's house.

"I have an idea," he said. "I think it'll give you a lot more time. Chris's parents will help you. Wilma, go with her."

"Nope," I said, folding my arms. "I came this far with you, I have to do the rest too. That's just how it works. I can't let you go back there by yourself. I would never get over it if I did that. Don't try to make me go to Nancy's house. I'm going to follow you anyway."

He just looked at me sadly. "Okay, if you insist. I don't like it, though."

"I don't like it either, for either of you. I think you should just come with me." said Julie, and when we said no, she shook her head as she walked away with the stroller and the toddler, adding, "Well, God will take care of you, I hope."

"Yes, He will," I added in a whisper.

Chapter Seventeen

Keep Your Head Together

Rodney looked at me and said, "Well okay, Super Girl, let's go fight Lex Luthor."

"So, what's your big idea?" I asked him as we walked back to his house for the third time.

"Let's get back to the house and I'll show you," he said, taking my hand. We walked along together, and the thought occurred to me that this might be our last time, walking down this road together, being thirteen and just enjoying our time. And all I did about that was just to try to really feel his hand on mine, how that was, and look around at the golden afternoon light on the trees, that looked like the most solid trees in the universe, and that Possumtown quiet to the air that didn't seem to happen anywhere else. A couple of times Rodney said something, and

I nodded, but I wasn't totally paying attention to what he said so much as the feeling of being with him and hearing his voice.

When we got to the house, Rodney threw the door open and called out, "Hey Mom, we're home," kind of like Desi Arnaz, and I had to laugh. "Hey, wait a second, Lucy, why you laugh like that," he said, still doing his Desi thing, and leaned me against the wall and kissed me. It was the best kiss yet, I was afraid my knees were melting, and then he said, "So, Wilma, you ready to meet my mom?"

"Ready as I'll ever be," I said, and followed him down the hall where she lay in her odiferous glamour.

"So, now I'm going to tell you what the plan is," Rodney said. "I'm going to pick up her head, and you're going to take her boots, and we're going to take her over there to John Smith's house, to meet him when he comes back. Except we're going to wedge the door shut and talk to him while he's still outside. I mean, I'm going to talk to him and pretend to be my Mom, like she's still alive and talking to him. He should go for it, he's been dying to talk to her all this time. But when he figures it out, we have to be prepared to run out the back and get away from there as fast as we can. Are you ready for that? It's not going to be easy. You can just stay here till it's over if you want."

"Nope, I'm going with you," I said. "Let's not talk about it too much, I got the idea. I'll hide in the back with you and run the same time as you except I'll go around the house, in the other direction, and cross the road and run for my bike. Hopefully he won't see me, but if he does it may distract him a bit, deciding who to go after first. Anyway, I can run pretty fast. Faster than a big old man like him."

"Don't do that! Just stay hiding. He will go after you if he sees you and he can really hurt you. I don't know if you get how dangerous this is. Maybe you should just go back to Chris' house."

"No way! Anyway, you need my help and we better work fast. I'll get her feet. Let's go."

"Okay, well then you better listen to me and just stay in the house, or else run with me if you have to, but don't run off by yourself like that, that's the worst idea yet. All right, let's get her."

Then looking at his mom, he said, "Okay Mom, we have to take you somewhere. Phew, you don't smell so good, sorry to say." He started to pick her up. She was light enough, but getting stiff, and her skin was soft and squishy. A liquid fell from her pants and onto the floor that smelled disgusting.

"Ew," I couldn't help myself, "what is that, poop? And I have to hold her feet?"

Rodney looked at me and laughed a little, and I just looked back and covered my mouth and nose with my hands. Then he said, "Phew, mom, I should have put a diaper on you. GG's would probably fit you too." Thinking for a second, he ran to GG's room, grabbed one of his diapers, and stretched it around her outside her pants. It helped, but some still dripped out over her boots. I said, "I can't put my hands in that. Tell you what, we'll hold up her head and her butt, and I'll take this side and you go on that side."

Rodney said, "I guess that'll work. Too bad we don't have time to clean up. Let's go," he said as we heaved her up, then squeezed our way down the hall and out the door. He decided to go straight through the bushes, and a stray branch almost pulled her scarf off, but he got it loose.

"Don't lose your scarf mom," he said, almost cheerfully, "you need it to keep your head together."

I had to laugh. "Yes, she does, but don't say stuff like that, I almost dropped her."

We got to John's house, took his mom into the living room, on the left, and plopped her down in the overstuffed chair that every living room seems to have. "I hope you can sit here, Mom. I think you'd fall out of the regular chair. I can't believe how stiff you are. How long have you been dead? Not even twenty-four hours yet."

I adjusted her scarf and sunglasses. "Hmmm. I wonder if John's wife left some lipstick behind. I will look around. Perfume too, because let's face it, she really smells."

We looked for a bathroom, then found it halfway down the hall that ran between the kitchen and the living room. We washed our hands, just because it seemed like a good idea, and looked around. A lot of pills that mostly neither of us recognized, although I thought I saw one that my brother Rick might have been taking. Some were big and scary looking. A lipstick in the cabinet. Pink. "That'll look nice with the blue scarf and sunglasses," I said.

We went back to the living room and put lipstick on his mom. "Looking a lot better now, Mom," said Rodney. "Now I better lock the door. You go behind the chair. It's getting a little darker, I'll leave one little lamp on and see how that looks from outside."

He turned on the lamp and went out to look in the window, creeping as quietly as he could even though John couldn't be back yet. Then we heard the truck. He slunk quickly back into the house, locked the door, then ran into the kitchen, grabbed one of those new chairs and wedged that under the door knob, then pushed a side board from the hall between the chair and the kitchen doorway, so it was as secure as he could get it. Just as he heard John getting out of his truck, he ran to the living room and hid behind the chair with me. We heard John trying to open the door. "Damn," John was saying, "where did I put that key?"

We were expecting that, because nobody around here locked their doors much. Rodney swallowed, took a long breath, and piped up, "Hey there, John," emulating his mother's voice, I imagined, in a weird contralto with a bit of flirt in it. "Hey John, you hear me alright? I heard you wanted to have a little conversation with me. What's it about?"

"Oh my god, Miranda, is that you in there?"

"Yes, it is. Who does it look like, Dolly Parton?"

"Ha ha, she doesn't have anything on you as far as looks go, Miranda. Too bad your kids don't look more like you. That boy of yours is like a stick insect with pimples."

"Never you mind about my boy, he does just fine, John Smith. I'm wondering about you. What are you doing here with this sweet young Julie, much too sweet for you, you rascal. She says you only got out of jail a little while ago."

"Where is she, anyway?"

"She's upstairs, putting her kids down for a nap. Whose kids are they, anyway? Not yours?"

"No, I don't even know the guy. Some character she took up with while I was in the big house. Some no-good alcoholic, like that guy who was hassling you last night. Hey, you know what's funny? That pony-tail guy is from Harrisburg, right? Happen to find out, he's the brother of my girl. She's always talking about him and what a great guy he was. She had no idea what he was up to. Why was he bothering you anyway?"

"Oh, he was such a dork. He wanted me to help him sell this whole big bunch of pills he got a hold of, but I can't do that with my kids in the house, you know. And then he told me I better not tell anyone about it, and I said, well I will if you give me anymore trouble, and that was a mistake. I forgot how nasty he gets when he's drunk sometimes," Rodney improvised.

"And he strangled you, well. I can't believe you're still with us. That kid of yours nursed you through it, huh?"

"Yes, but I'm still having trouble getting around. Listen, I have a few questions for you. You knew I didn't like you in high school, I guess. Did you know why?"

"Was it because of the time I kicked that stupid bulldog mascot and he wouldn't come out for the games anymore?" John asked, sounding contrite.

"No, although that was bad," Rodney said, not sounding nearly as appalled as he probably felt. "Just that you were mean to people just about all the time."

"There was that one friend of yours. Well, at least I didn't get her pregnant. Yeah, I knew you were mad about that," responded John.

I had to put my hands over my mouth again, and stared at Rodney, and he continued, "But even with all that, I could see that you kind of liked me."

"You could see that, really? I didn't think it was that obvious. But I guess you would have known that," said John, sounding sad.

"Yes, a person knows when somebody likes them. You can feel them looking at you and you kind of get that they are thinking about you," Rodney went on, rolling his eyes at me. I just stared back. I couldn't believe he could say all this stuff, so calmly. I was just hoping I wouldn't poop.

"That's a good thing though, don't you think?" said John. "I mean, weren't you at least a little bit impressed?"

Rodney looked back at me and responded, "Ahem. Well, you were always quite the character," and went on to ask, "So why, if you liked me so much, did you go on ahead and marry Julie? It's not as if you got her pregnant. Those kids aren't yours."

"The thing is, I always thought it was a huge cosmic joke on me, the way things turned out. I just married her because you were already married, and she was cute and seemed easy going, like she wouldn't make a problem about stuff. I was wrong about that, but anyway, I married her, just a registry wedding, you understand, and then it was only a matter of weeks later that I wound up killing your husband."

Chapter Eighteen

Her Beautiful Eyes

Rodney started, then he stared at me, gaping, with total lack of comprehension, kind of like when he saw me at his house for the first time on Thursday. *My God*, I thought, *he really didn't know how his father died. How could that be*? He looked like he was going to throw up. I just put my hand on his shoulder. His mom knew about this. Why hadn't she told him? To avoid scaring him? Well, that hadn't worked out too well. Then John said, "How in God's name could you have married that guy, right out of school, and everyone knew you made a big mistake. I got my mind made up that it didn't bother me that you wouldn't go out with me, but I couldn't believe it when I saw you were marrying that guy. I'm just glad I finally got the chance to tell you that."

Rodney put his hand on mine and started breathing. He took a second to swallow and take one more breath, then said to John, "First of all, I don't get it that you were so surprised. You knew we were dating. You probably even knew that I was pregnant. And he was nice to me, John, and mostly he was nice to other people too, when he wasn't too drunk."

"Oh God, Miranda, he was a mouth-breathing moron," replied John.

"And that's a reason to kill him?" Rodney's voice broke a little.

"Maybe you didn't know this, but he started showing up at the bait-store I was working at, drunk most of the time and trying to horn in on my partner's side business, dealing guns out of the back of the store. He said he knew everything about guns, too, just from being in the army. I'm a Marine. I know guns. Anyway, you don't just walk into a situation like that and try to push people around. You have to talk to people first. My partner was getting nervous and even said something about quitting, but we were making good money, so I didn't want to hear about that. I told him to leave it to me. I will say, I did try to talk your husband into leaving us alone, but he was joking around about ratting us out if we didn't cut him in. So, while he was checking out the merchandise out in back of the place, I let him have it. My partner helped me, but I shot him myself. We tried to make it look like suicide, but they wouldn't buy it."

Rodney piped up again, "Why would they think he killed himself? He had it made, living off me and my welfare money. Well, I knew it happened at that store, but I didn't know that he was trying to get involved in your little business venture. I wouldn't have let him even talk about selling guns. I honestly thought you killed him just because he was my husband, to get me back for ignoring you all those years."

I was wondering where the backdoor was and kicking myself for not checking.

"Well I would really like to talk with you about this face-to-face," said John. "I don't have the key, could you get up and let me in?"

"I'm sorry, I just can't get up right now. I guess I just can't get my breath."

"Where's my wife? Hey, Julie, come down here and let me in."

"You can't shout, John, you'll wake up the kids."

"To hell with that. Are they even up there? You better not be lying to me, Miranda."

"Keep your voice down, John."

But he started kicking the door in and the chair and table were shaking. Rodney grabbed my hand and we ran for the living room door, leaping over the furniture behind it in a scramble to the kitchen and saw the kitchen door almost at the back of the house. We were out of it in seconds, running through the scrub to Rodney's backyard and on into the next one. About that time, we heard a horrible wailing noise from that house. "Miranda, my God, what happened to your beautiful eyes?" John Smith was screaming. In a flash, my mind's eye saw what John Smith saw, Rodney's dead mother's once beautiful face a molten puddle with darkening dry marbles for eyes.

Rodney jumped when he heard it and fell over, getting a sneaker stuck on a bramble bush and having to leave it behind, limping a bit with one bare foot. This was my chance, and I took it, running across the road to my bike. "Wilma," yelled Rodney, "don't, please."

But I kept going, and then we heard John barreling out of the house and both took off our separate ways. I grabbed my bike and started dragging it to the road.

It was downhill from there, but I still don't know why I thought I could ride fast enough to get away from him. He had jumped in his truck, and as I got up steam, he came up behind me and rammed my bike. I went flying clear off, and it's a good thing I did because he ran right over it and smashed it to bits. Then he jumped out and ran over to me. He grabbed me by the arm and I screamed at the pain, realizing it must be broken. "Hurts, huh? Good," he grunted, and pulled me up and threw me bodily into the truck.

He grabbed some duct tape out of the glove compartment and taped my broken arm to the window crank. "Try to open it now," he said.

I was totally frozen with fear and sure that I had pooped myself by now, though I couldn't feel anything. "So, once I catch up to your little boyfriend, I'll kill you first. Just straightforward murder, nothing weird. I'm not interested in a kid like you, I like real women."

I just looked out the window, and then it was as if I was floating over the truck, looking down on the whole scene like it was a bad movie. He drove off and picked up speed, careening around the corner to the right, which was unfortunately where Rodney had emerged from running behind the houses. He was there, crouched over and breathless, and I tried to open the window and yell to him, but my arm hurt so much, and I couldn't get any sound out of my mouth anyway. I couldn't even breathe.

John got out of the truck and ran over to Rodney, bellowing like a Balrog from out of the Deeps of Moria. He picked Rodney up by the shirt as if he were a mop. "Was that you, in there? That was you talking? Making fun of me, pretending your Mom was alive, pretending to be her? Where's my wife? I knew they left. I got your little friend in the truck there. Now you better tell me where they are, you little stick insect, and then maybe I'll kill you both instantly instead of messing with you first."

Rodney just gaped at him, and then gasped, "Mom told me."

"Told you what?" yelled John, in disbelief, but curious in spite of himself.

"About the other people you killed." What? I just gaped at the both of them, and suddenly thought, wow, how many people?

"Oh yeah. I'll just bet she did. What did she know? About her husband she knew, sure, but what else did she say? If you know all about it, who was it then?"

"Police," blurted Rodney.

"Well, dang, maybe she did tell you something. How on earth could she have known? Yeah, it was a cop all right. He was tailing that father of yours, and he came running into the shop right after I nailed your dad. So weird that nobody found that cop, but they got me about your stupid, insignificant Daddy. Now it's your turn to die, just make it easier on yourself and tell me where my wife is."

Rodney just opened and closed his mouth, and John roared at him and lifted him a foot higher. As he did so, the policeman who was running up the sidewalk, with another two right behind him, grabbed John's arm and pulled it behind him, putting a gun to his back and yelling "Police."

John dropped Rodney, raised up his arms and staggered back a step. Another policeman caught up, and as they were cuffing him, Rodney said to John, after coughing and catching his breath, "That's what I was talking about. The police are coming."

I was only just barely able to take in what was going on, and it wasn't until then that I realized Rodney had been bluffing. Behind the police car, Chris's dad, Al, pulled up in his car and came out, looking for Rodney. He walked around the police cars and I saw him hug Rodney and I think Rodney burst into tears. "We called the police as soon as Julie explained to us what was going on," Al said. "Thank God they got here in time. Rodney, I don't know how you did it."

When Rodney stopped and wiped his eyes, Al looked him in the face and said, "You don't have to do this all by yourself anymore. We're going to help you. Okay?" He hugged Rodney again and then ruffled his hair.

Rodney laughed, "I think my dad used to do that," and almost started crying again.

"Why don't you sit in the car," said Al. "I'll go talk with the police, and I'll ask them if we can take you back to the house."

Rodney started for the car, and then said to Al, "Uh, wait a second. Wilma is in that guy's truck."

"What?" said Al, "Oh my God, we thought she went home. What did he do to her?" and they both came running over to the truck where I was still sitting with my broken arm.

"I was wondering when you would remember about me," I said to Rodney, somewhat scornfully. "No, don't open the door," I said to Al, but he did it anyway, and I screamed like a heifer being slaughtered. "Oh my God," I cried out, "you're going to pull my arm off."

"I'm so sorry, Christ, Wilma, I really am," said Al, staring at my arm taped to the window crank. Rodney just came up with tears in his eyes and started pulling the tape off, slowly. "Did he hurt your arm doing that?" asked Al.

"I broke it," I said, sobbing, "when he knocked me off my bike."

"Oh my God," said Al, and turned and called to the police, "we need an ambulance for this girl. You guys gotta call an ambulance, she broke her arm and God knows what else happened to her," he added, looking pale.

Then to us, he said, "If you got her arm off of there, Rodney, why don't the two of you come sit in the car and I'll turn the heat on. You look like you're freezing all of a sudden."

Both of us were shivering, and we went, going around the police cars and not looking at John Smith. We sat in the car and tried to keep breathing. After doing that for what seemed like an hour, Rodney said, "Wow. The ponytail guy, my mom, my dad, some policeman. His parents too, maybe. I hope nobody else is dead."

Al came back. "They said they can talk to you Monday. Tomorrow being Sunday, they don't want to bother the girl who types out everything, so they said Monday's better. Plus, you get a chance to rest. You ready for dinner? Pretty soon!"

Rodney just looked at him, then presently said, "Dinner, wow."

"Yeah, just wait. Barbecue ribs and macaroni with cheese, with green beans and corn, and apple crumble with ice cream for dessert."

Rodney giggled. I said, "I don't know what my parents will want me to do. Probably go home."

I turned and looked out the window, away from them. Meanwhile, Al added, "They said this guy may have killed more than just the one he went to jail for?"

"Yes," said Rodney, "that was my dad, too."

"I didn't know that. I'm so sorry."

"Yes, thanks. Yes, and besides my dad, he shot the blond guy who killed my mother, and a cop. And, the blond guy is Julie's brother, or so said John. Do you think we should tell her?"

"Oh, well," said Al, "you know, she was in a hurry to get back to Harrisurg, and some friend of my wife's was going there, so she took them. I would let someone else take care of that. Yeah, just your family and mine in the house tonight, and you guys can stay as long as you want. Plenty of room in the basement. Meanwhile, I guess the police contacted Wilma's parents, and her dad is on his way over. I guess he wants to take her to the hospital himself."

So we sat in the car, and they talked, and I stared out the window, until a policeman walked up. He was a middle-aged man with a worn-looking face, and he said, "I just wanted to check on these two brave kids. Young lady, your father should be here soon. We're about to take Mr. Smith into custody. By any chance, would either of you like to say anything to him?"

Rodney shook his head no, but I turned around from the window, probably crying, and said, "Yeah, I think I would like to say something to Mr. Smith if that's alright."

The policeman said, "Come with me, young lady," and went around the car to open the door for me. He walked me over to the police car where John Smith was sitting in the back with handcuffs on. He was looking out the other window, stone-faced, kind of like I was in Al's car. The policeman said,

"Excuse me, John, but this young lady has something she wants to say to you."

He grunted, and sort of half turned around, without looking at me, but I could see he was listening. I cleared my throat a little, like Rodney said I always do, and said, "Mr. Smith, I think I forgive you, because I get that your life has not been that great, but you need to learn another way to deal with it when you feel bad." Then I wheezed for a minute or so.

He grunted again, "Hmm," then added, "so what do you suggest? Suicide?"

I got my breath and said, my voice clearer now, "I suggest Jesus. When I feel bad, I talk to Him, especially if I know nobody else is going to listen. Sometimes I get up real early and watch the sun come up, and I talk to Him then, and sometimes the day is still lousy after that, but I can get through it a little better after talking to Him. It's not exactly your fault that you didn't know that, but I wish someone would have told you before you killed a bunch of people."

He just sat there, and after a minute of that, the policeman started to lead me away. As I was leaving, he said suddenly, "Hey, kid."

I turned around, and he was looking at me this time, and he had tears in his eyes.

"Thanks," he said. I started crying too, and I just waved to him. The policeman said, "Good for you, John," and led me back to Al's car.

I asked him, "Did you know John Smith?"

He looked down and said, "Yes, it was me who arrested him all those years ago. And you know, he has had a tough life. That was well said, young lady."

Just then, my Dad's car pulled up. He jumped out, and even though it was a Saturday he was wearing a blazer, though a slightly informal one that looked a bit worn. Al and the policeman both came over to him, looking concerned, and maybe a little anxious to please. For some reason, people in Possumtown tended to act that way around Dad. He had a sort of air of authority, that he may have picked up from leading his unit in the Bulge. And being almost Paul Newman handsome didn't hurt. Too bad Gil and I were basically average, but I covered all that before. Anyway, on this day, Dad had a look I rarely saw on him, which was fear. And that scared me, because when Dad got scared, he usually got angry too. "Officer," he greeted the policeman, ignoring everyone else, "can you tell me what happened?"

He put his hand on my shoulder but barely looked at me. The policeman, who was younger than Dad but looked like he had seen a few things, took a few seconds to think before he answered, looking at Dad in a sort of unfocused way, and smiling a little, reminding me of Rodney. "Well, Mr. Wilson, we're not sure of all of it, and I guess we won't hear all the details until Monday. But you should be very proud of your daughter, who has been through a lot to help her friend who was in certain danger, that young man in the car over there. His neighbor was a convicted murderer who was menacing their family, and if Wilma hadn't shown up when she did, things might have gone a lot worse for them."

"I see," said Dad, and then he turned to me and asked, "when did you leave the house?"

"Last night," I said, no longer feeling like I wanted to lie about it.

"This is the kid you were talking about after the library? This is what you did when I didn't want to go straight over there? You just took it in your own hands?"

"You didn't want to help," I said, clearly and without apology. I looked at him then. "I couldn't wait, because Rodney needed to know what I found out. And his mother died."

"Officer," my dad said, "people died last night? My daughter was in danger?"

The policeman hesitated for a second, then said, "She did put herself in harm's way, but she did it to help her friend. I think she showed a lot of courage."

"She's thirteen years old," my dad said to the policeman.

"Yes, I understand," said the policeman.

My dad looked away for a minute, then looked back and said, "Well, thank you for letting me know. I am going to take my daughter to the hospital now."

I looked at him for a few seconds, then said "Bye" to the policeman and Al, with Rodney in the car who may have heard me, or maybe not. My dad pushed on my shoulder to get me to leave, and I said, "Ow!" and went with him to the car. No apple crumble for me.

My dad was completely silent until we were almost at the hospital. Then he said, "You need to know that we have changed plans, your mother and Gil and me. Instead of bringing Gil over to Europe with me, I am taking you. I don't think having a broken arm should make a difference, once it's in a cast. I will handle the bags. I just don't think you should be here any longer when you might run off and get yourself in trouble again. And we are leaving tomorrow morning."

I just looked out the window and didn't say anything. I was crying, but I didn't want to make a big deal out of it. If he was going to act tough, well, I could do that too. And I wasn't too surprised that he had made some awful decision that ruined everything. It had begun to seem like that was what my parents could be trusted to do.

I barely remember the hospital. The doctor made some bad joke about whether my nose had been broken and not fixed correctly. I barely heard him. I kept thinking about missing Rodney and the kids at dinner that night, and for every night or day in the future, seemingly. I still hadn't shown Nina how to make bathrobes for her Barbie dolls. I pondered these things, and I kept up the silent treatment. I had nothing to say to Dad, anyway.

We got home, and I could tell Mom had been crying, and that made me feel sad for about five minutes, until I came to see how pleased she was that I would be leaving and out of her hair. She offered to help me pack, and I said, no, I could do it, and she said what about your arm, and I said not to worry. She helped me get started anyway, and she was amazed that I didn't want to bring hardly any of my books. The only ones I took were *The Hobbit* and *The Lord of the Rings*, which back then were published in three separate paperbacks, and my Zondervan Bible that they gave me when I joined the Presbyterian church back in Philadelphia. She promised to keep the rest of them in storage.

I asked my mom, "Could I call Rodney and just tell him that I'm leaving?"

She took a breath and looked at me, and said, "I suppose that would be okay. Just don't take long."

I went to the phone. I had to look in the phone book to find Nancy and Al's number. I dialed it, and Nancy picked up. "Are you okay, sweetie?" she asked, "did they take care of you at the hospital? Is your arm better?"

I said yes, and I asked how Rodney was doing. She said, "You know, he was so tired after dinner that I'm pretty sure he's asleep, and I would hate to wake him up. That might be good for you too, to get some rest."

Without crying, I said, "That's too bad. I have to go to England with my Dad tomorrow morning. I wanted to tell him about it and say bye."

She breathed in sharply and said, "I can't believe he's making you do that. Al said he did look really upset. I'm so sorry to hear it, I'm sure you would have liked to spend some time with your friends before you went so far away. Just a minute," she said and put the phone down.

I heard voices in the background, Al and Rodney talking about something and laughing, and I thought, *he's not asleep at all*. After a while she came back to the phone and said, "I just wanted to check and see if he could talk to you, but he can't, honey, I'm sorry. But just think, before too long, I imagine you'll get the chance to come back and visit. You'll see him again, and the babies, and Nina and Dan, and us. This isn't the end."

I had to take a minute to keep from sobbing, and said, "Tell them good-bye for me, okay?" and then I got off the phone.

Before I went to bed, I took most of the clothes out of my bag and made sure it was good and light. Then I slept. But I woke up very early, as I sometimes used to do, while the sky was still dark. I think I already mentioned how I loved to go out to the barn to watch the sun come up, and if they heard me, that's what they may have thought I was doing. My dad was right, having a broken arm didn't get in the way that much, since I carried my bag on the left and it wasn't that heavy. I decided to take Old Mill Road down to the main road. I had no taste for going down Creek Road again, and it wasn't the way I wanted to go anyway. Instead of hiking all the way down to Nancy and Al's house, I stopped and turned left at the A&W. With the sky beginning to turn light, I walked another 15 minutes to my friend's house, and knocked on the door. There was Mary, and behind her, her husband, Gus. He took one bleary look at me and went straight to the stairs and called up, "Lucy, wake up and come down here, you need to see this."

Mary just took my bag and said, "Come on and sit down, dear, and I'll get you some coffee," with one of her best smiles.

Then Lucy, blinking with sleep, peeked in the kitchen and said, "Oh my God, Wilma, I thought you were on your way to England by now," and I finally burst into tears. She came up and gave me a hug and her mom handed me some tissues. When I calmed down a little, I said, "Lucy, he doesn't really love me."

She said, "Probably not. But we do."

Epilogue

That's pretty much the end of the story of what happened that spring of 1973. My Dad wound up taking my brother Gil to England that morning, and I think they were both pretty happy about that. My Mom relented about letting me stay until the end of the school year, but after that, we went to England too. We left my brother Rick in some sort of program where he got help from caseworkers and had a job and an apartment, but that didn't last long. He said somebody spiked his drink at work, which could be true. Anyway, after a period of homelessness, he wound up in a Catholic worker home near Syracuse, similar but bigger than the one where Aunt Donna worked. He liked it there, and he managed to stay there for a pretty long time, for him.

Nancy and Al got appointed guardians for Rodney and his brothers and sister, and they stayed on, living with Nancy and Al and their kids, and eating Nancy's wonderful cooking. For them, life got better, but of course Rodney could never forget what he had been through. We stayed friends, and we wrote sometimes after I left. We never talked about it, but we had a sort of truce. I guess I understood, somehow, that he had been through too much to deal with having a girlfriend, especially since I was getting ready to move so far away.

The thing about Rodney, though, is that he did bounce back, better than I ever did, or so it seemed to me. I was happy to see that, but a bit jealous too, and I often wondered why. And I may or may not be right, but I came to think that it was because he was still living in Possumtown. In 1973, that place had a quality to it that will never be seen on this Earth again. Part of it was the profound quiet. This was best enjoyed on a farm in the back country or up in the mountains, but back then, any average Possumtown citizen had access to this profound quiet that could save a person's soul. And the beauty of the place, the whir of thousands of grasshoppers surrounding Possum Lake on a summer afternoon, the singing of the first bird when the gray mist of twilight turns pink with dawn, the shining of a dew-covered cobweb in the sun, these things made Possumtown what it was.

Of course, Rodney thought it was boring there, and was jealous of me for getting away, but I believe now that he was the lucky one. But that was another thing that we never talked about, so I don't know if he understood that or not.

By the way, just in case anybody wants to know, that book I used to carry around was *Look Homeward, Angel* by Thomas Wolfe.